TELL-ALL
Nell Carson

New York City writer Kat Callahan is just finishing an explosive unauthorized biography of Hollywood's golden couple, Alex and Victoria Janssen, when they mysteriously disappear along with their 7-year-old son. Kat's publisher is hot on her heels to complete the book, eager to cash in on the free publicity surrounding their disappearance.

Little does Kat know, the charming cowboy who's just strolled into her life is actually Alex Janssen's brother Luke, dead-set on stopping the book. He knows it will reveal a fiercely guarded secret that could destroy the lives of all four Janssens. Now he'll stop at nothing to ensure that doesn't happen.

TELL-ALL
•
Nell Carson

AVALON BOOKS
NEW YORK

Published by Thomas Bouregy & Co., Inc.
160 Madison Avenue, New York, NY 10016

Library of Congress Cataloging-in-Publication Data

Carson, Nell.
    Tell-all / Nell Carson.
        p. cm.
    ISBN 978-0-8034-7754-4 (hardcover: acid-free paper)
    1. Women biographers—Fiction.   2. Motion picture actors
and actresses—Fiction.   3. Married people—Fiction.
4. Family secrets—Fiction.   I. Title.
    PS3603.A77625T45 2010
    813'.6—dc22

                                          2009045424

PRINTED IN THE UNITED STATES OF AMERICA
ON ACID-FREE PAPER
BY HADDON CRAFTSMEN, BLOOMSBURG, PENNSYLVANIA

To Shelly—thanks for everything!

Chapter One

"It's a very powerful virus, very cool. I've never seen anything like it."

Kat Callahan saw a nearly lascivious gleam in the eyes of Benny Simons, Winslow Publishing's "Information Systems Manager," a grandiose title for a guy who looked as if he graduated from high school last week.

She took in a deep, calming breath. "Yes, Benny, I get how 'rad' it is, but can you fix it?" Benny didn't seem to hear her, he was so intent on the virus.

His manner had changed dramatically from Tuesday, three days earlier, when Kat had first brought in her laptop. That morning she'd opened the file containing her manuscript only to see garbled text where before there had been close to 85,000 painstakingly selected words.

At the time Benny had been confidently indifferent about the laptop, focusing more on Kat.

He'd even attempted the old pickup routine countless men had tried—"Let's try to name your hair color"—along with the usual guesses: auburn, copper, ginger, burgundy.

In fact, her hair, long, thick, and wavy, had strands of all those colors and more. Not liking the attention her hair drew to her, Kat sometimes felt tempted to buy a box of Mousy Brown #109 and be done with it.

Now Benny sat back in his chair, shaking his head in admiration. "It reached into every corner of the CPU, the flash drive—even the power source is affected." He peered up at her through thick glasses. "All that and it's absolutely undetectable even with the latest scan."

"Well, yippy-dee-doo. Don't I feel special?"

"I found the culprit, an e-mail from Victoria Janssen." Benny lifted an eyebrow at Kat. "You know, you really should be more careful opening e-mails from people you don't know."

"Maybe I *do* know her." She felt as if she did anyway, after months of research on the A-lister and her equally famous husband, Alex—together Hollywood's Golden Couple for the last decade.

Winslow had commissioned Kat to write an unauthorized biography on the Janssens after receiving a juicy tip about the paternity of the couple's seven-year-old son, Jeremy.

Now the company was chomping at the bit for the

book's release, wanting to cash in on the media frenzy for all things Janssen.

Three weeks ago Alex Janssen had walked off the set of his latest movie without a word of explanation. Since then no one had seen or heard from him, Victoria, or their son. The entire populace of the United States was now utterly obsessed with finding them.

Benny raised both eyebrows skeptically. "You know Victoria Janssen? Right. Seriously, though, hackers love to use famous names. Unless you know for sure it's to you specifically by the subject line, don't open it, especially any attachments."

"There *was* no attachment on that one." Kat hated the defensiveness in her voice, but she just felt so dumb about the whole thing. When she'd gotten the e-mail, supposedly from Victoria Janssen, she'd opened it immediately, thinking the woman had finally responded— and *personally*—to Kat's many requests for information from her publicist. It had made her feel big-time—a feeling that quickly deflated once she discovered that the e-mail was only a method of delivery for some nasty little virus.

"Well, I'm sure a lot of people fell for it." Benny's green eyes sparkled, and he leaned closer to her. "But, hey, if you really *do* know Victoria Janssen, try to find out where she's holed up. *Juicy Weekly*'s paying twenty-five thou' for any word on her, Alex, or Jeremy. *Each*."

"So I hear," Kat said, her patience growing short. She didn't have time for this. She was booked on the red-eye to Denver tomorrow night and hadn't even started packing—assuming, of course, that this all worked out and she could actually go. "Seriously, though, can you fix it?"

"Sorry, there's not a lot I can do. Don't you have a backup?"

Kat shook her head. "Just what was on the flash stick." Unfortunately, the virus had infected that as well.

As to another copy of the file, she'd e-mailed the nearly completed manuscript to her editor, Brian Winslow, two months before, and he'd given it back to her with extensive editorial comments and suggestions. She'd spent the last month making Brian's revisions, but since, then, at the request of—no, under the *command* of—"Upstairs," as everyone called the bigwigs on the top floor, she had not printed it out or e-mailed it. Upstairs was concerned about the story's leaking out before the book's release. Heck, they were downright paranoid about it.

Brian wasn't going to be happy about the delay making the revisions again would cause, not to mention the impact it would have on her dream vaca—Oh, Lord. Kat's stomach lurched when she remembered what *else* was on the laptop. "Are you—" Her voice squeaked, and she swallowed hard and began again. "Are you telling me that *all* the files on my computer are gone? Irretrievable?"

"Yep. Sorry."

Damn. The Janssen book could be remedied, although she hated the idea of making all those revisions again—

not to mention what that would do to her vacation plans. What she couldn't take was the thought of the *other* file's being gone, her *real* book, a novel called *The View from Here*. She'd been working on it since college— nearly a decade's worth of work.

Helpless, frustrated tears welled up in Kat's eyes, and she squeezed her eyelids shut, squelching them.

Benny must have sensed her distress and took pity on her. "Look, I have a friend—" He paused, stood, and scanned the sea of cubicles surrounding them. Motioning for her to come closer, he continued in a whisper, "I have a friend in the Village who might be able to help. He's got a bootlegged prototype of a new data-retrieval program that's supposed to knock the socks off Data-Back's latest version."

Kat closed her eyes and took in a deep breath, willing back a semblance of patience. "In English?"

Benny flashed her a sheepish smile as he sat back down. "Sorry. It's a program that can take whatever remains from your damaged files and rework it, filling in gaps and sequences in the data until you have something very close to the original material."

"*Close*?" Kat instantly regretted her scoffing tone when she saw the affronted expression on Benny's face.

"Well, fine, if that's not good enough . . ."

"No, I'm sorry. Please, Benny, what's the address?"

As he wrote down the address and phone number of his friend, Benny glanced back up at her. "By the way, I got it—your hair color." His lopsided grin was apparently intended to be seductive but missed its mark by about a continent. "It's like a sunset blazing in the western sky."

Kat forced a smile. He was trying to help after all. "Thanks," she said, taking the slip of paper. "I owe you one."

"No problem-o." Benny winked at her. "And just so you know, I'm always up for a drink after wor—" His eyes suddenly widened, and he sat up straighter.

Kat felt a touch on her arm and turned to see Brian Winslow smiling at her, the overhead lights reflecting in his designer glasses. As usual, not one hair was out of place, and his suit was wrinkle-free despite its being close to the end of the day.

"Got a minute?" Brian asked.

"Sure." Kat turned back to Benny. "You'll get that spare laptop ready for me?"

"Yes, Miss Callahan, right away." Benny bobbed his head up and down several times fast, clearly nervous. Brian was, after all, the grandson of the company's CEO. He could be intimidating too, an air of old money surrounding him like expensive cologne.

"Thanks," Kat said.

As Brian steered her toward his office, he leaned in close, a snide grin curling up one side of his mouth. "So, should I be jealous?"

Kat looked at him, confused. "What?"

"Benji back there. I heard him mention a drink."

Kat let out a breath. "His name is Benny, Brian, and I thought we agreed to keep it—"

"Yes, yes, *light*—I know," Brian said, his voice tight. "I was just kidding anyway." His petulant frown made his already boyish face appear even more childlike.

Across town, Luke Janssen set his suitcase and duffel bag down in front of the door to Kat Callahan's condo. "Lucy, sit," he ordered the black Lab beside him. But Lucy was having no part of it, her attention focused on the bit of black nose poking out from under the door. That had to be Oliver, Callahan's yellow Lab.

Both dogs whined and scratched at the bottom of the door, anxious to meet in person, so to speak. "All right, all right, hold your horses, you two."

Juggling the key and Lucy's leash, Luke finally managed to unlock and open the door. Lucy let out a happy yelp and nearly knocked Luke over in her excitement to get inside.

Watching the two Labs warmly greet each other, taking whiffs of all the requisite hello-doggie parts, Luke hoped Callahan didn't rely on Oliver for any semblance of security.

After dragging his bags into the condo, Luke was about to close the door when he glanced over at the door across the hall. It was slightly ajar. He caught sight of one blue eye peering out through the crack before the door closed quickly.

He shrugged, went back into the condo, and closed

the door. Stepping over his bags, he walked in and sat down on the couch. He pulled his cell phone out of his jacket and pressed 1 on his speed dial. A moment later a silken voice breathed "Hello" into his ear.

"It's Luke. I'm in."

The voice let out a throaty chuckle. "My, how dramatic. So, how is it?"

Luke surveyed the condo, taking in the antique-looking furniture and knickknacks, the Victorian wallpaper, and the Oriental rugs. "Looks like an old lady lives here." But then he saw several abstract art pieces hanging on the walls that clashed with the rest of the decor. "An eccentric old lady."

"Hmm, interesting."

Luke let out a breath. "Well, I'd better get started. I have a lot to do."

"Is it there?"

Luke looked over at the desk by the far wall where a stack of yellow lined paper lay ready for destruction. "Yep."

"All right, then. Go to it."

Luke grinned and saluted the phone. "Yes, ma'am."

He hung up the cell and put it back into his pocket, then headed to the desk, nearly tripping over the two dogs still reveling in each other's company. Lucy barked as she play-nipped Oliver's ear. Oliver twisted around until his paws were on Lucy's head. Lucy yelped again. "Cool it, guys," Luke said, but he was, of course, ignored.

* * *

Kat followed Brian through his office door, his name elegantly etched in the glass. Framed book covers lined all four walls. Brian walked behind his mahogany desk and sat down, gesturing toward one of the plush chairs facing him.

Kat sat down and sighed at the tabloid magazines strewn across the top of Brian's desk—Victoria, Alex, and their son, Jeremy Janssen, plastered on every cover.

"So, what's the verdict?" Brian asked.

"He can't fix it, but he gave me the name of a friend of his he thinks can help."

Brian's brow creased. "Oh, I don't know, Kat. You know how Upstairs feels about outsider involvement in this."

Kat raised her palms in frustration. "It's their paranoia that got me into this trouble in the first place! If I could have printed it out as I went along like I wanted to, or e-mailed it . . . God, four weeks of revisions! If this doesn't work, there goes Colorado."

It was to have been her reward to herself for getting her first book published. An entire month in the glorious Rocky Mountains. The year before she'd done an article for *Dog's Life* magazine about a Web site that organized vacation swaps of places welcoming large dogs. She'd decided to try it for herself and her beloved yellow Lab, Oliver.

After registering her condo on the site, she'd periodically checked the available spaces. She'd been thrilled when a foreman from the Shallow J ranch high in the

Colorado mountains signed up, wanting to swap his cabin for a place in New York City for a month. Perfect. But now that was all in jeopardy.

Brian got up and walked around the desk, sitting in the chair next to Kat's. He put a sympathetic hand on her forearm.

"I'm sorry, honey. Really. But you know how important this book is to Winslow. And the timing is so great! Have you seen these?"

He gathered up the tabloids on his desk and fanned them out in front of her, the banners blaring out all the rumors swirling around the Janssens' disappearance: *Jeremy Kidnapped! Janssens Join Cult! Aliens Abduct Janssens!* The last was Kat's favorite. Supposedly, the aliens had mistaken the Janssens for leaders of the planet because of their worldwide fame.

"I know, it's ridiculous," Kat said, shaking her head.

"It's free publicity is what it is."

Brian held up *Juicy Weekly,* the top-selling tabloid Winslow Publishing secretly owned through a subsidiary. "The reward was Dad's idea." Kat glanced down at the cover—*Where Are They?* emblazoned across a picture of the Janssens, the offer of the twenty-five thousand at the bottom.

"So you can understand why Upstairs wants the book out ASAP," Brian said, his eyes glistening with greed. "Marketing's working overtime. They're planning a rushed release once the DNA results come in."

"*If* they come in," Kat said dryly.

"Oh, no, nothing's going wrong this time. Dad put a security detail on it. And the lab said they're getting close. So once we have that duck in the row, the rest are going to have to line up real quick. How's that last chapter coming?"

Kat gave him an acerbic chuckle. "Just 'ducky.' I wrote it out by hand after my laptop got sick. Benny's lending me another one, so I'll type it in tonight. Then, assuming his friend fixes the old file, I'll add the last chapter and be done tomorrow. And I'll be on the plane by eight. If he can't fix it, though . . ." Kat let her voice trail off ominously.

"Well, let's just think positively."

Brian looked down at the magazine in his hand, the cover shot showing Alex holding Jeremy on his shoulders with Victoria walking alongside, smiling up at both of them.

"The 'First Family of Hollywood,' " Brian scoffed. "God, the hypocrisy." He peered down, focusing more closely on Jeremy. "He sure does look a lot like Alex. If I didn't know better . . . She really could have pulled it off."

Kat sighed, also looking at the handsome little boy, a tuft of his thick brown hair falling across his laughing face. She glanced at Victoria, taking in the absolute adoration in her stunning eyes as she gazed at her husband and son. The muscles in Kat's stomach tightened uncomfortably.

"Brian . . ."

Brian didn't look up at her but began leafing through the magazine. "Hmm . . . ?" When she didn't continue, he glanced up at her, saw her troubled face, and lay the magazine back down on his desk.

"Is all that still bothering you? I thought you were okay with it by now."

"He's only *seven,* Brian. It's not his fault his mother—"

"No, it's not his fault," Brian interrupted. "But it's not *our* fault that they put us into this position. They *use* us, Kat, parading him around in plain sight, soaking up the publicity when it's convenient for *them.*"

"I don't think they parade him around, exactly. Just going to the store, for instance—"

"Don't be so naïve, Kat. They have a dozen Mr. Becks and Miss Calls to do just that. No, it's a chance to be *seen,* to show off their 'perfect little family.'"

Kat's shoulders sagged as she leaned back in her chair, already sensing defeat but not quite ready to give up. Although she knew how futile these discussions were, pressing these points made her feel somehow better about the whole thing. "But maybe they're just trying to be normal."

Brian huffed out a breath of irritation. "Kat, look. I'm sorry you're still having these feelings." His expression softened. "I actually think it's sweet of you to care about them like you do. It's one of the reasons I—"

Oh, God, don't say it, Kat thought. Too late, she realized she'd winced. Instantly it registered on Brian's face, his jaw stiffening. "Really, though, at this stage in the game . . . I mean, you're almost done with the thing, for crying out loud."

Kat nodded with a slight shrug, hoping to appease him. "I know, you're right." She forced a smile and looked down at her infected laptop. "Well, I'd better get this over to Benny's friend so he can start doing whatever he's going to do to it."

Brian nodded, his mouth remaining a tight line, and stood up to walk her to his door. "So, will I see you tonight?"

"Oh, I don't think so, Brian. After I type in the last chapter, I still have to pack. I'll call you when I hear from Benny's friend, okay?"

"All right."

Kat felt his eyes on her as she walked back over to Benny's desk to pick up the new laptop.

She was going to have to do something decisive about Brian when she got back from Colorado. Despite her attempts to keep things light, he'd gotten increasingly more possessive. Still, she dreaded it. She knew he wouldn't take it well.

Brian Winslow was used to getting his way.

The man in the blue Windbreaker leaned against the building, his eyes intent on the tall redhead across the street. Oblivious to him, she walked out the glass doors of the fancy-schmancy high-rise, *Winslow Publishing* printed on the awning in swirling green letters.

The man glanced up at the dark clouds gathering

overhead and pulled the hood of his jacket up around his face as the first drops fell. He took a sip of cold coffee from his Styrofoam cup, pulled out his cell phone, and pushed the redial button.

"It's me," he said gruffly into the phone. "Alice has left the tea party. Repeat, Alice has left the tea party."

An impatient rush of air came through from the other end. "Spare me the drama, okay?"

The man huffed. "It's code, not 'drama.' It helps to—"

"Fine. Thanks for the update. Call me the second she gets off the sub—"

"But I was about to go home," the man interrupted, his officious tone dropped in favor of a high-pitched whine. "It's raining. Can't you just—"

"Look, I don't care if a friggin' Category Five hits. Just do your job."

Now it was the man's turn to let out an irritated breath. Unfortunately, the line went dead mid-sigh. No satisfaction.

He took one last sip of coffee, then threw the cup at the trash can by the curb. Of course he missed.

Luke Janssen put down his cell phone, shaking his head. If there was one thing he hated more than yellow journalism and summertime in Manhattan, it was incompetence from his employees.

He should have fired that so-called private investigator the first time he'd switched on the whiny mode. It made the man sound like a five-year-old.

Knowing time was short, he got back to the matter at hand, ripping sheet after sheet of yellow lined paper into tiny unreadable pieces, taking tremendous satisfaction in the sound of every tear, knowing each one helped delay the publication of that wretched book.

Chapter Two

K at climbed the steps of The Ramparts, the imposing turn-of-the-century building she'd lived in since
she was ten. The five-story whitewashed stone struc-
ture loomed overhead like the defensive wall of a castle.

As usual, Kat had to jiggle her key in the lock of the
main door before it finally gave in and opened for her.
None of the other residents had problems with the
lock—only Kat, as if the building itself had never truly
welcomed her.

Once inside, Kat walked through the dated lobby toward the elevator, thankfully standing open. She stepped
inside and pressed 3.

"Hold the elevator!"

Wonderful.

Kat held the doors open and smiled politely as Mrs.

Burgstrom, her elderly next-door neighbor, a deceptively frail-looking woman, stepped into the elevator, clutching her ever-present Siamese cat, Walton, tightly to her chest.

"Good afternoon, Mrs. Burgstrom, Walton," Kat said, the false cheerfulness in her voice sounding transparent even to her.

Mrs. Burgstrom had been her grandmother's closest friend and confidante. Ever since her grandmother's death, Mrs. Burgstrom had seemed to take on the task of making Kat feel inadequate and guilty, constantly emitting an air of vague disapproval just as her grandmother had done for so many painful years.

"Ah, Katherine," Mrs. Burgstrom began, and Kat cringed, sensing trouble in the woman's voice. She sighed, resigned to her captive-audience status and pushed 3 again, willing the elevator to hurry up. Of course it seemed to operate in slow motion now as the doors took their own sweet time reclosing.

Mrs. Burgstrom patted Walton's head, as usual a little too hard, and peered up at Kat through her small gray eyes. "I'll have you know your dog woke me from my nap *again* today."

"But he hasn't barked in—" Kat protested, but Mrs. Burgstrom silenced her with a single raised finger, a familiar gesture and one Kat had learned to despise.

"Well, he barked today, and louder than ever. I thought you should know I'm writing yet another letter to the co-op board. And rest assured, this time they *will* take action."

"Oh, please, Mrs. Burgstrom, don't do that yet," Kat pleaded. "Give me a little more time to train him."

Kat's dog, Oliver, a huge yellow Lab, was the most good-natured and adoring dog on the planet but not exactly the sharpest knife in the drawer. After failing to curb his barking by any conventional training methods, in desperation Kat had purchased a contraption called BarkNoMore, a collar that emitted a supposedly harmless electric current every time he barked. But Kat had felt so guilty each time she used it, she'd shower affection on him until it finally dawned on her that she was actually training him to bark *more*!

She'd gotten more serious about it lately and no longer babied him. And it was working. Oliver hadn't barked in several weeks—until today, apparently. Kat sighed again, realizing she'd have to turn up the intensity of the current.

But Mrs. Burgstrom was shaking her head resolutely. "I *am* sorry, Katherine, but I'm quite at my wit's end. I have given you plenty of chances. Enough is enough. I'm ill, as you know, and my doctor has given me strict orders to get as much rest as possible."

Kat stifled an urge to roll her eyes. Mrs. Burgstrom had been "ill" for the twenty plus years Kat had known her.

"Please, Mrs. Burgstrom," Kat begged again as the elevator reached their floor.

"I'm sorry, Katherine, but my decision is final." With a dismissive turn of her head, Mrs. Burgstrom stepped off the elevator. Kat let out yet another exasperated breath as she watched the old woman make her way down the hall, emphasizing a limp Kat knew came and went, depending on who was watching.

Shaking her head in defeat, Kat headed toward her own condo. Passing Mrs. Burgstrom's, though, she couldn't help sticking her tongue out as the woman closed the door, an admittedly immature gesture but satisfying nevertheless.

Kat was just about to put her key into her lock when the door across the hall opened. Great. She just wanted to get inside and relax for a minute before she began typing in the last chapter.

"Howdy, neighbor," Jackie Southland greeted her brightly. Jackie, a widow in her early thirties, wore a denim miniskirt with brown cowboy boots, emphasizing her long, lean legs.

When she'd moved in, Jackie had told Kat she'd been training to be a beautician but dropped out when she married the school's eighty-two-year-old founder. He'd died a year after the wedding, leaving his grieving young widow a lucrative chain of beauty schools.

Jackie had offered Kat numerous makeovers, but Kat had always refused, slightly offended at being deemed needy of one. Besides, she wasn't too big on makeup. She didn't even own any except for one tube of lipstick, a shade darker than the natural color of her lips, and some dark brown mascara.

As a teenager she'd tried various products to cover up

the many freckles spattered across her nose and cheeks but had long since given up. By midday the makeup had always faded, the freckles shining victorious and resplendent like a small universe of brown stars. Her mother had called them God's kisses, sporting her own set proudly.

"Hi, Jackie," Kat said, pleasant enough but trying not to encourage her.

"So, anyway," Jackie began, cocking her head to one side, as usual not one lacquered hair moving out of place. "I was thinking you and your friend should come over sometime for cocktails. Tonight maybe?"

Her key in the lock, Kat turned, confused. "I'm sorry, who?"

Jackie's hand flew nervously to her neck, her inch-long scarlet nails scratching just under her ear as she feigned nonchalance. "Your, uh, man friend?"

Oh, Kat realized, *she must be talking about Brian.* He'd been over a couple of times. Was Jackie interested in him? It seemed like it, the way she was fishing for a date.

Kat didn't think Brian would be interested in Jackie. She was a little . . . much. But that wasn't for her to decide, was it? Besides, setting him up with someone else would make it crystal clear she wasn't interested in pursuing anything further with him.

"Sure, Jackie, that sounds like fun. I'll ask him. Not tonight, though, okay? I've got a lot to do."

Jackie's overly plucked eyebrows dipped in disappointment, but she gave a light shrug. "Oh, okay. Some other time, then?"

"Definitely," Kat said with a smile as she turned the key in the lock.

Putting her purse and laptop down on the padded bench in the foyer, Kat took a couple of deep breaths and frowned. What was that smell? Oliver came lumbering up to her, and Kat bent down distractedly to pet his head. "Hi, sweetie."

The smell intensified as she walked down the short hallway to the living room. It was a musky scent, unmistakably masculine. She stopped suddenly. Had she been robbed? And by a freshly after-shaved burglar?

Hesitantly, Kat took several more steps inside. And then she saw him, stretched out on her living room couch, strong bare arms clutching her grandmother's afghan to his chest, a beige cowboy hat tilted down, covering his entire face.

"What the—" Kat began, but before the words were out of her mouth she knew the answer: Tanner McIntyre, the cowboy from Colorado. A day early!

"Some guard dog you are," she muttered down at Oliver, her eyes still on McIntyre.

At the sound of her voice he'd stirred, and he now reached up and pushed back the cowboy hat, blinking up at her in sleepy confusion.

Involuntarily Kat drew in a sharp breath at the sight of his face. He was the quintessential Marlboro Man, only younger, his face deeply tanned and perfectly chiseled, full lips slightly parted above a strong chin. Pronounced cheekbones, angling out above a couple of days' growth of beard, set off his cornflower blue eyes, slightly down-turned at the very edges. That seemed somehow wrong to her, the shape of his eyes, but Kat had no idea why. He reminded her of someone, though, didn't he? She couldn't quite put her finger on who, but whoever it was, their eyes weren't down-turned like that. Great. Now it was going to bug her.

Understanding finally cleared the man's thickly lashed eyes, and he grinned. "Hey, it's the city girl," he said, his deep voice gruff with sleep.

His terminology rankled Kat, and she opened her mouth to tell him so but closed it immediately when the cowboy took in a deep, cleansing breath, stretched his arms out to either side, and sat up, the afghan falling completely off, revealing his broad, naked chest.

Appalled at where she suddenly found her eyes, Kat quickly averted her gaze back upward to the safe zone of his face.

But it wasn't safe at all, Kat realized immediately, seeing the small, knowing smile rise up on his lips.

"Well, now, I didn't expect to meet the city girl," McIntyre said, those same two words grating on Kat. She sensed he knew it and had done it on purpose, teasing her. How dare he! He didn't even *know* her! This time she would not be distracted.

"My *name* is Katherine Callahan, not 'the city girl,'"

she stated firmly, pleased at how strong and determined her voice sounded.

McIntyre's lips parted in what Kat now recognized as an amused smile. Perfectly even white teeth gleamed in contrast to his tanned face. Heck, couldn't he at least have bad teeth?

McIntyre dipped his hat in obviously insincere contrition. "Pardon me, ma'am. Sure is nice to meet you. I'm—"

"You're *early* is what you are," Kat finished for him, a shade too sharply, perhaps. She was just *so* not in the mood to deal with this. "You're supposed to be here tomorrow night."

McIntyre's eyebrows again dipped in confusion. Kat saw then that his nose angled slightly to the left. At last, a flaw!

"Come again?"

"To-mor-row," Kat repeated slowly and clearly, her jaw clenched tightly, she realized. She loosened it, refusing to let this ill-mannered cowboy or his aw-shucks act get to her.

Without an ounce of self-consciousness McIntyre stood up, dressed only in Levi's faded close to the color of his eyes.

Kat's gaze flicked back up to his face, and she saw that same slow grin creeping across those firm, Harrison Ford lips. He'd caught her wandering eye once again— the second time in under five minutes!

Kat drew in a calming breath as McIntyre muttered,

"Well, I got the fax of our agreement right here." He reached for the back pocket of his jeans, inadvertently—or deliberately, for all Kat knew—thrusting his chest out as he reached back, muscles flexing everywhere but especially emphasizing the rock-hard six-pack of his stomach.

Too slowly he slipped the folded fax from his pocket. "You know, come to think of it, I was a bit surprised that your dog was still here. I thought you might've just plumb forgot him!"

Refusing to be baited any further, Kat nodded down at the battered piece of paper in his hand. "The fax, Mr. McIntyre?"

"Tanner, please. Only my cows call me mister." Kat rolled her eyes at that, but Tanner was looking down at the fax as he unfolded it. "All right-y then, let's have a look-see, shall we?" He studied it for a moment, then let out a surprised little grunt. "Well, lookie there, that *is* a three, ain't it? And here I was thinkin' it was a two."

Taking a step closer to her, Tanner pointed to the paper. "See how light this here loop-ti-loop is?"

Kat saw his point and nodded. She realized she was holding her breath, trying not to inhale the musky scent of him.

Thankfully he took a step back, refolding the fax. Giving her a teacher-to-slow-student look, he admonished, "Maybe you should write a little more clearly next time, ma'am."

Kat felt her jaw stiffen again. "Please don't call me ma'am. It's Kat."

Again with that irritating grin. "Like the animal?" And then, unabashed, he began a slow appraisal of her, his eyes traveling from her face all the way down to her toes.

"Are you done?" she asked pointedly, planting her hands on her hips.

With a decisive nod he declared, "Yessiree, it suits you, your name. Kat. Long and lean and just a little bit mean."

Kat forced a quick, terse smile. "Do you think it would be possible for you to get a hotel room for the night?"

Tanner chuckled. "No can do, ma'am—Kat. There's an International Kennel Club convention goin' on this week. You should-a seen all them pooches in the airport. I reckon every 'doggie' hotel in town's been booked for weeks."

Kat's shoulders dropped in resignation. "Well, it's just one night, I guess."

Tanner dipped his hat. "Mighty obliged."

Kat frowned suddenly, looking around. "Where is your dog anyway?"

Tanner nodded at the closed bathroom door. Oliver was lying down in front of it, sniffing under the door. "In there. She's being punished."

And then it dawned on her. "*You're* why Oliver barked. He must have, when you came in!" *Good.* Now she wouldn't have to turn up Oliver's collar. She'd have to explain the situation to Mrs. Burgstrom, tell her it was a one-time thing. It probably wouldn't make a shred of difference, but it was worth a try.

"Oh, no, ma'am—Kat," Tanner was saying, "your dog didn't let out even a yelp. I was surprised at that, I have t'say. Never met a dog that didn't bark when a stranger came in unexpected-like."

Kat planted her hands on her hips again. "So it was *your* dog that barked? Didn't I tell you that quiet was absolutely essential? Or wasn't that clear on the fax either?"

With a shrug, Tanner answered, "Well, I didn't think it applied to the dog!" He chuckled again. "I mean, you can't exactly teach a dog not to bark."

Kat stood up straight and again put her hands on her hips. "You most certainly can! Oliver is wearing a special collar that gives him a little zap every time he barks. It conditions him not to bark."

Tanner's thick eyebrows dipped down. "But that's like teaching a coyote not to bay at the moon. It's . . . unnatural."

"Well, it's very natural in New York City." Kat let her arms fall to her sides in exasperation. "Your dog woke up my neighbor Mrs. Burgstrom, and now she's writing a letter to the co-op board. And this time they're going to 'take action,' whatever that means, but it can't be good!"

"Sorry again, ma'am." As Tanner dipped his hat once more, Kat bristled in irritation.

"It's Kat, and aren't you supposed to take that thing off inside or in the presence of a lady or something?"

Tanner shrugged good-naturedly. "I sure will if you want me to." Reaching up, he pulled the hat off in a smooth, casual stroke, and instantly Kat wished he'd put it back on. Rich brown curls sprang down, framing his face, the dark strands, together with his thick lashes, accentuating the blue of his eyes, making them . . . breathtaking.

Kat had always liked blue eyes—or any color eyes for that matter, except brown. Her genes had not been programmed with the striking green eyes of her mother's but the boring brown of her father's.

Her sister, Andrea, had inherited the green eyes, and Kat had always been so jealous, especially when Andrea laughed, her eyes sparkling like two emeralds glistening in sunlight. Lord, she missed the sound of that laugh. Sometimes she heard it so clearly in her mind, it seemed real, as if Andi were right there. . . .

"I'm sorry if I offended you, Kat," Tanner was saying, suddenly closer to her than he had been. She took a quick step back. How long had she been standing there, her mind swimming in twenty-year-old misery? She hated when those memories snuck up on her like that, out of nowhere, once again ripping open the wound that never seemed to heal.

"You didn't," Kat said quickly. She didn't like his expression—all the smugness and arrogance gone—now filled only with compassion, as if he'd been reading her thoughts.

Kat looked away from his now too-expressive blue eyes, her gaze falling to his chest. She frowned. "And do you think you could manage to put a shirt on?" Trying to instill severity into her voice, she'd failed miserably, the words sounding only weak and pleading. And suddenly tears were close, her emotions completely out of control. But really, it was understandable, wasn't it? Around this time of year, especially *this* year . . .

"Well, all right," Tanner said softly with a small nod. He turned away from her, bent down to pick up a white T-shirt from the arm of the couch, and slid it on. Tucking the shirt in under his belt, he gave her a quick grin that was obviously intended to lighten the mood. "Boy, you city girls sure are partic-u-lar."

Just then a scratching noise, followed by a whimper, came from behind the closed bathroom door. Thumping his tail against the floor, Oliver looked up hopefully at Kat and Tanner.

"Why's your dog being punished anyway?" Kat asked. "Did he and Oliver fight?"

"Nope," Tanner replied with a fond smile aimed toward the bathroom. "And he's a she." Frustrated, Oliver stood up in front of the door, looking from Kat to Tanner, his warm brown eyes pleading.

Tanner went over to him, leaning down to pet him, scratching up against the fur on the back of his neck, then back down. Oliver's tail swung happily back and forth. He had obviously fallen in love with the man.

"And they got along just fine. Like two peas in a pod. Isn't that right, boy? Yep, just like that, two peas."

Kat's frown deepened. Was he stalling? Tanner glanced up at her, and, seeing her quizzical look, his eyes darted quickly away. Kat's stomach tightened as she recognized his expression. Guilt.

Instinctively her eyes went to her desk in the corner and widened in disbelief. Where there should have been a neat half-inch stack of yellow lined paper, there were only two sheets!

"Oh, my God," Kat whispered, her gaze falling to the trash can now filled with finely shredded yellow paper.

The last chapter.

It looked like a huge tub of popcorn. The pieces weren't much bigger than that, Kat saw as she walked over to the corner and collapsed onto her knees. She plunged her hands down into the mass of yellow, her fingers clutching the tiny shreds covered with the disjointed swirls of her handwriting like an impossible jigsaw puzzle. His dog was more efficient than a shredding machine!

"I'm so sorry about this," Kat dimly heard from behind her. "I only left her alone for twenty minutes or so while I took a shower." Kat released the handful of paper and sat back on her heels. She closed her eyes, trying to regain a tenuous hold on her temper, her fingers curling up into fists so tight, the nails dented her palms.

"I guess it's being in a new place," Tanner continued sheepishly. "I thought she was over that."

In a rush of new anger, Kat finally lost the battle over her temper, and she banged her fists on the floor. "Well, you thought wrong, didn't you?" she spat out at him, her eyes narrowing. Kat had the satisfaction of seeing McIntyre wince.

As she stood, Tanner took a wary step back. As well he should. "Do you know what this means?" she asked in a low, menacing voice, her jaw tight. "Do you have any idea?" Wisely, Tanner remained quiet and only shook his head slightly, looking ready to run at a moment's notice. "I'm going to have to stay up all night to redo that chapter. All night!"

Tanner raised his palms in supplication. "I'm so sorry. If there's anything I can do . . ."

"Oh, you've already done *plenty,*" Kat snapped.

Tanner gave her a long, appraising look and then nodded slightly. "All right, then," he said quietly. "I'll just stay out of your hair. If you like, I could rustle us up some dinner."

"I'm not hungry," Kat said curtly.

"Well," Tanner began in a logical tone, "if you're going to be up all night, you'll be needing something to keep you going." With that, he escaped into the kitchen.

Coward, Kat thought, but she felt her anger dissipating as more pragmatic thoughts took over. First of all she needed to be more comfortable.

Heading into her bedroom, she changed into sweats and a T-shirt and swept her hair up into a ponytail.

She emerged in slightly better spirits. After all, she did know the chapter backward and forward, having spent the last three days polishing it. Still, though, she thought with a glare toward the kitchen, she hated having to reinvent the blasted wheel.

After putting on a pot of water for the angel hair, Luke ducked into the guest room, picked up his cell phone from the nightstand, and pressed 1.

"It's Luke. Just checking in. How's everything?"

"Fine, just fine."

"Good."

"Is she buying it so far?"

"Seems to be."

The voice let out a throaty chuckle. "So, 'Tanner,' what do you think of her?"

Luke smiled. "She's one tough cookie, all right."

"Ah," the voice murmured, "a challenge."

"That, my dear, would be an understatement." Luke envisioned Kat Callahan when she'd first squared off at him, hands on hips, strands of that glorious red hair framing her beautiful, freckle-splashed face, her deep brown eyes trained solidly on him. He'd liked the way her chest had heaved with emotion, daring the world— or maybe just him—to take her on.

He knew it had been a risk, acting the way he had— the whole cocky-cowboy routine—but he'd gone with his instincts. "Nice" wouldn't have cut it. A woman like Kat needed a challenge, someone she could sink her teeth into. Now that he'd caught her attention, though, maybe it was time to try a different tack. Keep her guessing, keep her interested. Anything it took.

Anything.

The man standing across the street in the Windbreaker looked from the front window of Callahan's condo up toward the sky, the stars winking out one by one as rain clouds moved in for one more round.

No way was he hanging around for this one. His jacket was still damp from the earlier shower. Thanks to this awful job he'd learned the difference between water-resistant and water*proof* cloth.

No, he'd played chump long enough. Besides, why did he need to keep track of Callahan when Luke Janssen was right there in the same place with her?

Shivering in the chilly night air, he made his way down the street toward the closest subway station.

Chapter Three

Tanner set a steaming plate down next to the computer along with a glass of Shiraz and silverware tucked into a napkin. "Sorry, the spaghetti's a little skinny. Maybe I didn't cook it long enough."

Kat couldn't suppress a laugh. "It's angel hair. It's *supposed* to be 'skinny.'" An embarrassed grin curled Tanner's lips. "Sorry I laughed," Kat said, still smiling but honestly trying not to.

She felt much better now. She was pleased with how the chapter was going. It seemed to flow easily, almost writing itself. Actually, she had to admit, it was better than before. She'd added a paragraph where she now realized she'd needed to expand on a thought and had deleted two others, one redundant and one unnecessary.

And at the rate she was going, she already knew she wouldn't have to stay up all night.

"Just so you know," Tanner began in a quiet, sincere tone, "I really am sorry about what Lucy did."

"Oh, dogs'll be dogs," Kat replied with a light shrug. "And I'm sorry I came down on you so hard from the get-go. I've had a bad couple of days and took some of it out on you."

Tanner grinned. " 'Some'?"

"Okay, a lot. Thanks for being my surrogate punching bag."

"Anytime."

"And thanks for this," she said, nodding down at the plate heaped with the "skinny" spaghetti smothered in a rich marinara sauce she'd forgotten she had.

"No problem," Tanner replied. "I was going to make a salad, but I couldn't find the fixin's. You don't shop much, do you?"

Kat shook her head, thinking of her near-empty refrigerator. "We're pretty much a city of take-out addicts," she explained. "In fact, I could probably name every single Chinese restaurant between here and Lex."

Tanner shrugged. "Well, I'm sure that would be mighty impressive if I knew what a 'Lex' was."

Kat laughed. "You'll learn. Thanks again for making this."

"Thank *you* for understanding about—" Tanner's eyes widened. "Lucy!" He rushed over to the bathroom door and flung it open. Oliver leaped up from his bed in the corner as a streak of black came bounding out of the bathroom. The two dogs scrambled happily toward each other, toppling over one another in the center of the living room. Lucy let out a joyous yelp.

"Lucy, shush," Tanner ordered, and Lucy obeyed instantly and padded over to him. "You horrible beast, you got me into big trouble," he muttered, sinking his fingers into her thick, shining fur. "I hope you learned your lesson. I am sorry I forgot about you, though." He nuzzled his face against her head. "I'm a terrible parent."

"She's beautiful," Kat said. Noticing Kat, Lucy turned to her and, tail wagging, came over to meet her. "Hi, girl." Kat petted her the same way Oliver liked. Maybe it was a Lab thing, because Lucy obviously loved it too.

"Come on, you," Tanner said, grabbing a dark blue leash from the coffee table and clipping it on to Lucy's collar. "Time for walkies."

" 'Walkies'?" Kat laughed but then felt bad when she saw his embarrassed smile again. "Sorry. It's cute, is all."

"Love being called that," Tanner said, grinning. "You want me to take old Oliver too?"

"Sure, thanks. His leash is in the bowl by the door. Remember to take a newspaper bag for the—"

"Oh, I know all about that," Tanner cut in as he found Oliver's bright red collar and clipped it on, then grabbed a blue newspaper bag from the bowl. "My sister, Luanne told me about your pooper-scooper law."

He shook his head, steering the two dogs toward the door. "You city folk sure got some odd notions."

And then they were gone, the two dogs disappearing in a swirl of black licorice and butterscotch.

Kat drank the last sip of her wine and yawned. The glass of Shiraz and the mountain of pasta had made her sleepy. She needed to get up and move around, get her blood flowing again. Besides, she should check in with her houseguest.

She was glad they'd been able to have a somewhat fresh start after their unfortunate first meeting. He'd been considerate too, taking Oliver along for his nightly walk. And after they'd come back, Tanner had put them both in his room so they wouldn't disturb her work.

Now Kat stood, arching her back to alleviate some of the stiffness there. She picked up the empty plate and glass and headed into the kitchen. Tanner was leaning over the dishwasher, looking inside intently.

"Oh, hey," he said, smiling at her and glancing down at the dishes. "I was just going to get those for you." He nodded toward the dishwasher. "Are these clean?"

"Yes, but don't worry, I'll do it," Kat said, putting her dishes into the sink. "You cooked, I'll clean. Universal roommate rule. I need a break anyway."

"I don't mind helping," Tanner said. "Besides, I'm still feeling the need to do penance for my mutt's evil doings."

"All right," Kat said with a light shrug. Together they put the dishes away, periodically mumbling "excuse me" to each other as they navigated the tiny kitchen, really only big enough for one person.

Kat had to admit, though, she liked the little tingles that swarmed across her skin when Tanner lightly touched her arm or the side of her waist to reach around her. There was nothing wrong with being attracted to the man after all. It wasn't as if anything were going to happen. Their situation made that impossible.

They began doing the dinner dishes, Tanner rinsing them off and handing them to Kat to put into the dishwasher. After a few moments Kat became acutely aware of the silence between them.

"So," she began, surprised at how shy her voice suddenly sounded. "I guess it's not very busy on the ranch this time of year? I mean for you to be able to take so much time off."

Tanner nodded. "The herd's still down in the low country. Now it's just a waitin' game for the snow to melt. Then we drive 'em on up for the summer."

"Snow?" Kat asked, thinking about what she'd planned to pack. She hadn't figured on snow. "So it's still cold out there?"

"Oh, yeah. Don't forget, you're going to be more than eight thousand feet above sea level. It's always colder at that altitude. The sun's a lot stronger up there too, though, so during the day it can get pretty warm. Just wear a lot of layers, and you'll be fine."

Tanner smiled then. "This is a great time to visit the Shallow J. The air's so fresh and clean up there." He stopped, taking in a deep breath through his nose as if smelling the Colorado air right there in her kitchen in the middle of Manhattan.

"I can't wait for the cattle drive. It's my favorite time of year—the open fields, the blue sky against snow-capped mountains so close, you feel like you can touch them. And when we're campin' at night, it's so quiet, the only sounds are the coyotes, the cracklin' of the camp-fire, the leaves rustlin' in the aspens overhead."

Kat sighed, seeing his contented smile. When was the last time she'd looked like that?

She leaned over to put the last pot into the dishwasher.

"Ow," she heard as her ponytail whipped around and struck Tanner across the cheek. She hadn't realized he'd also bent over to put the forks into the silverware basket.

"Oh, sorry," she said.

"What'd I do to deserve that?" he asked, rubbing his cheek. "I'm sorry if I wasn't fast enough with the sil-verware."

Kat laughed, but her smile faded as she became aware of his proximity to her. And she was trapped. If she took a step back, she'd trip over the dishwasher door. He was so close, she could feel the heat of him through his T-shirt, smell his intoxicating, musky scent.

As if in slow motion, she watched his hand come up, saw his fingers twirl around a loose strand of her hair by her temple. "You've got *some* hair there, little lady," Tanner said softly, his gaze moving from the curl of hair to her eyes.

A little unsettled by the intent way he was looking at her, Kat swallowed hard. "I, uh, better get back to work," she said awkwardly.

"All right-y then," Tanner said, still holding her eyes. "I'll make some fresh coffee and bring it out to you."

"Wow, what service," Kat said, looking away from him with a shy laugh. She suddenly found it difficult to maintain eye contact with him. Instead, she looked down at the soft whiteness of his shirt. She couldn't remember the last time a man had unnerved her like this, if ever.

"We'll think of a way to tip me later," he said in that same soft voice.

Kat looked up at him sharply and saw that slow smile again, his blue eyes twinkling. He pulled his hands away and raised them defensively. "I'm joking, Kat. But, seriously, how do you like your coffee?"

"Just cream's fine," Kat said. Bending down to close the dishwasher, she let out a breath. She needed to get a hold of herself. She had zero time for distractions.

"Here you go," Tanner said a few minutes later, handing her a mug. It smelled unusual, but she couldn't quite place it. "Cinnamon," he explained. "Tillie, our cook at the ranch, makes it like that, and I guess I'm addicted."

Kat took a sip, and the pungent richness of it brought to mind chilly winter evenings spent in front of a fireplace. "Mmm, I like it."

"Good. Well, I guess I'll be turning in."

"Let me know if you need anything. There should be fresh towels in there. Oh, and there's a TV, but the walls are pretty thin, so if you could keep the volume—"

"Actually, I was wondering if I could borrow a book or two?"

Kat didn't realize until it was too late that she'd raised her eyebrows in surprise.

He gave her a frank look. "We *do* read up in them thar hills, you know. They done learnt me my numbers and letters real good-like."

Kat gave him a sheepish grin. "Touché."

Taking a sip of the deliciously different coffee, Kat watched Tanner walk to the shelves stacked floor to ceiling with the books her mother had collected over the years. When he reached up to pull a volume out from the top shelf, his shirt rode up a few inches from his jeans. Kat let out a breath and looked back down at her laptop. *No distractions, no distractions,* she chanted silently to herself.

When he came back over to her a few moments later, Tanner was holding two books. Kat read the spines—*A Separate Peace* by John Knowles and a book of short stories by D. H. Lawrence. Although Kat would have pegged him for a Hemingway or London fan, she knew better now than to voice her stereotypes.

Tanner stopped, smiling broadly, his teeth so white against the tan backdrop of his face. "And, hey, if I do happen to make too much noise, you *will* tell me, right?

I mean, you won't go zapping me with that collar contraption in the middle of the night?"

Kat returned his smile. "I promise I'll give you plenty of warning."

She watched him walk toward the guest room, his stride radiating confidence. She definitely liked the way he moved.

No, she chastised herself, *don't think that way.* She'd be gone tomorrow and would never see him again. There was absolutely no sense getting all . . . whatever she was getting about him.

With renewed resolve she took another sip of coffee, turned back to the laptop, and got to work.

Chapter Four

Kat awoke to the delectable scent of a toasted blue-berry bagel. "Good morning," she heard from behind her.

She opened her eyes to see the bagel, smeared thick with fluffy cream cheese, next to the computer, along with a mug of that delicious cinnamon coffee.

Kat lifted her head up off the desk and instantly winced, raising a hand to massage her sore neck. "I'm too old for all-nighters."

She heard Tanner chuckle softly as he walked closer to her. "Yes, you're ancient. Here, let me." Placing his hands on her shoulders, he rubbed his thumbs deeply into the stiff muscles of her neck.

"Mmm," Kat murmured, cradling her head in her arms, "perfect."

"Sorry to wake you. I didn't know how much more you needed to get done."

"No, I appreciate it."

"Do you have a lot more to go?"

"Just a couple more pages," Kat replied, raising her head back up. Tanner pulled his hands away. "Thanks for the massage." She nodded down at the bagel. "That too." Picking up the bagel, she smiled up at him. "How did you know that's my favorite?" She took a bite, the bagel still warm, the soft cream cheese melting into the crispy top—just how she liked it.

"I don't know," Tanner said with a shrug, sitting on the couch and unrolling the newspaper. "I guess something about you just screams toasted blueberry." He took a bite of his own poppy-seed bagel. "Mmm, good stuff. My sister told me I had to try an authentic New York City bagel. I was going to just go to the place next door— Westside Bagels, I think it's called?" Kat nodded. "But then Ernestine—"

"Ernestine?" Kat burst out, almost choking on her bagel. "You mean Mrs. Burgstrom?"

"Yep."

Kat groaned. "Oh, no. You didn't go bothering her about bagels, did you? I'm in enough trouble with her as it is."

But Tanner was shaking his head. "No, you're fine. As I was locking your door, she opened hers to get the paper, and her cat ran out. I caught him. And I've got the scars to prove it." He raised his left arm. Three ugly red lines ran from the inside of his wrist nearly to the elbow.

Kat winced. "Ow. I don't blame him, though. I'd try to get away from her too."

Tanner gave a light shrug. "I don't know. She was nice enough to me."

" 'Nice'?" Kat repeated, incredulous.

"I thought so. I introduced myself and asked if she could recommend a good place for bagels. She told me I should go to Elmo's a block over. Apparently," he continued, putting the paper down and raising his finger in perfect imitation of Mrs. Burgstrom, "Elmo's puts the *proper* amount of sesame seeds on their bagels, *and* they whip their own cream cheese. They *don't* use the store-bought kind, unlike Westside. I have been instructed *never* to go there, not under any circumstances, no matter the bagel emergency."

He dramatically wiped the back of his hand across his forehead. "Phew, I sure did dodge a bullet there. I owe a lot to your Mrs. Burgstrom."

"Yes, you do," Kat said, laughing.

Tanner sat back again and gave Kat a quizzical look. "You know, I brought her back a bagel—sesame seed, of course—and it was as if I'd brought her a diamond necklace, she was so grateful."

Kat shrugged, considering that. "I guess we just don't *do* that kind of thing."

Tanner frowned. "Y'all aren't too neighborly around here, are you?"

With a wry chuckle, Kat replied, "Welcome to the big city." She took a sip of coffee. "Everyone sticks to themselves more or less. I mean, I'm friendly with a couple of my neighbors but not what you'd call close." She thought of Jackie and realized at that moment it was Tanner she'd wanted to have over for cocktails, not Brian.

Tanner refolded the paper and stood up. "Well, I guess I'll get out of here and let you get to work." Tanner nodded down at the dogs, both lying in front of the TV. "Them dogs and me were thinkin' about taking a nice long walk in that big ol' park y'all got somewhere 'round here."

Kat couldn't help grinning. "Central?"

"That'd be the one," Tanner said, walking to the foyer and picking up his cowboy hat from the bench. He put it on and grabbed the leashes from the bowl. Both dogs instantly jumped up and scurried over to him, their tails wagging in perfect unison as he attached their leashes. Tanner dipped his hat at her before letting himself be hauled out the door by the impatient dogs.

Kat grinned as she sat back down at the laptop, thinking how his cowboy getup was sure to attract attention. She knew intuitively that he wouldn't care. In fact, she wouldn't be surprised if he single-handedly started a trend and she came back from Colorado to see cowboy hats and boots popping up all over the city.

A couple of hours later Kat closed the laptop in frustration. She was on the last paragraph now but couldn't remember how it ended. She'd had the wording down perfectly in the handwritten draft.

Deciding to let her subconscious mind work on it, she stood up and stretched her arms out above her head. A workout would be a good break. Kat changed quickly into a pair of shorts, a running bra, and a tank top. Grabbing her kickboxing gloves, she headed out the door.

She opened it to find Mrs. Burgstrom standing there, one arm holding Walton, the other raised to knock. Kat was startled at her sudden appearance but even more surprised to see the woman actually *smiling* at her—not the curt, dismissive one Kat was used to but a full-blown, sincere, genuine smile.

"Oh, hello, Katherine," Mrs. Burgstrom said, her tone warmer than Kat had ever heard. "I'm so glad I caught you. I just wanted to let you know, you don't have to worry about that silly old letter I was going to write."

"I don't?" Kat asked blankly, wondering if the alien pod people from the movies had come to earth after all and landed in Mrs. Burgstrom's condo.

"Oh, no," the older woman was saying. "Your young man explained it all to me."

"My young . . . ?" Kat began, stepping out of her apartment and locking it behind her.

"My, my, a real cowboy all the way from Colorado," Mrs. Burgstrom said, stroking Walton as they walked down the hall. "What a charming, *charming* young man. And so considerate. I can't tell you how glad I am he'll be here a whole month. I simply must have him over for tea. The rest of the girls will just *love* him."

Her mind obviously on the cozy little get-together, Mrs. Burgstrom walked into her apartment, seeming to have forgotten all about Kat.

"Well, thank—" Kat began, but she found herself talking to a closed door. For a moment she stood frowning at it. *She'd* never gotten tea. What made *him* tea-worthy? Not that she'd enjoy it, but for Mrs. Burgstrom to invite Tanner McIntyre after just one day when *she'd* lived next door to the woman for twenty years!

Jackie's door opened then, and inwardly Kat groaned. She was in no mood for her.

"Hi again," Jackie chirped from her door. "I thought I heard you out here."

Overly made up as usual, Jackie wore a short, frilly bathrobe and clear, high-heeled slippers complete with pink pom-poms. They actually made those in real life? Kat had never seen them outside a Barbie dress-up set.

"Going for a workout?" Jackie asked, looking at Kat's outfit. Kat nodded, suspecting the woman had never done one sit-up or leg lift in her entire life. She'd probably been born with those long, sleek, model-like legs, unblemished by the ridges and bulges of muscle that marked Kat's own legs. "My goodness, you have a lot of energy for so early in the morning."

Kat frowned, looking at her watch. "It's ten o'clock."

"It is?" Jackie asked with a too-casual flip of her hair. "Well, it's early for me. I just got up a little while ago."

"Really," Kat said, unable to conceal her skepticism. It had to take at least a couple of hours for Jackie to get fully into costume including hair and makeup.

"Uh-huh," Jackie said evasively. She obviously had something on her mind. "So anyway, I was getting my paper this morning, and I ran into your friend Tanner."

Ran into? Kat thought, envisioning Jackie in her Barbie outfit, peering through the peephole of her door like a predator, waiting for Tanner to emerge so she could sink her talonlike nails into him.

"Wow, a real cowboy, huh?" Jackie was saying. "And his name, it's so . . . I don't know, leathery."

Kat raised her eyebrows, urging the woman to spit out whatever it was she wanted to say.

"Anyway," Jackie continued, her nails flitting around her neck in her nervous way, "he explained what you're doing, the whole vacation swapping thing—what a cute idea by the way. . . . And so," she began again quickly, apparently getting the message after Kat planted an impatient hand on one hip.

"I just wanted to check with you. I mean, you're not interested in him or anything, are you? I mean, he *is* pretty sexy. I could see where you might . . ." She laughed nervously. "I don't know, make an excuse to hang around a few more days? I mean, *I* would, if I were you."

"No, Jackie," Kat answered tersely. "I'm not interested in Tanner. In fact, I'm leaving later today. He's all yours."

Jackie's arms fell to her sides in obvious relief. "Oh,

great. I just didn't want to, you know, create any friction between neighbors." Her mission accomplished, Jackie turned back to her condo. "Oh, and have a fun workout!" she called behind her.

"Fun" was not what Kat had in mind as she began smacking the punching bag a few minutes later at her gym, her fists flying in hooks, jabs, and uppercuts. After a grueling series of roundhouses and back kicks, she stopped and leaned over, putting her hands on her knees to catch her breath.

She'd thought an intense workout would help alleviate some of the irritation she'd felt after the unpleasant encounters with her two neighbors, but it had only added fuel to it. She couldn't stop feeling as if everyone—Mrs. Burgstrom, Jackie, Tanner—couldn't wait for her to leave so the *real* fun could begin. Right now, she felt . . . superfluous. She knew it was irrational, but she couldn't help it.

Oddly, at that moment the final sentence of that last troublesome paragraph came back to her, word for word.

Good, she thought, untying her boxing gloves and yanking them off. Now she could finish the book and finally be on her way to Colorado.

And out of everyone's collective hair.

"Hey," Tanner said, looking up at her from the book he was reading on the sofa.

"Hi," Kat said tersely, heading straight for the laptop

on the desk. She wanted to type in the paragraph before she forgot it again. Putting her boxing gloves down next to the laptop, she frowned. Hadn't she closed the screen before she'd left?

She turned toward Tanner, who had gone back to reading his book. "Did you—" she began, but just then the phone rang. Leaning over, Kat picked it up from the console on the desk. It was Tad, Benny's computer friend from the Village.

"Is my computer ready?"

"No, uh, sorry, there was a glitch."

"A glitch?" Kat asked sharply. "Define 'glitch,' please."

"A problem with the program," Tad explained. "We're working on it, but it's going to take awhile."

Kat sat down, resting her forehead on her palm, already feeling defeated. "How long is awhile?"

"The rest of the day probably."

"Damn, damn, damn," Kat muttered.

"Sorry," Tad said again, meekly.

Kat felt bad for being snippy with him. "No, it's fine. I really appreciate your help. Call me when you know anything more."

"Will do."

Kat hung up the phone, sighed, and walked over to Tanner. "Well," she began, collapsing into the armchair, "it looks as if it's my turn to beg lodging for the night."

Tanner laid his book down on his chest and gave her a sympathetic look. "Problem?"

"Uh-huh," Kat said, nodding resignedly. "I have to

wait for my computer to be fixed, and he said it'll probably take all day. Good thing I rushed getting that last chapter done. Hurry up and wait. Oh, I'd better change my flight."

As Kat stood up and walked back to the phone, Luke shook his head, angry with himself. It had been unbelievably careless of him to leave the laptop screen up. He hoped Kat had been distracted by the phone call and would forget about it.

He'd have to be much more careful. At least Tad was on game. He'd liked the kid, even though he hadn't been able to convince him of the superiority of Data-Back's retrieval program over the one the kid had bootlegged from Japan. It had been an interesting debate, though.

And, judging from her side of the conversation, Kat hadn't suspected a thing.

Luke knew he'd only delayed things again, but at least it was something. Still, he needed to do more. Destroying that last chapter, sabotaging the DNA samples, and e-mailing the virus had all helped, but he needed to come up with something more than just another delay. That book needed to be stopped. It could never be published. Never.

He'd caught a lucky break finagling his way into Kat's life, and he intended to put it to good use. Emotional blackmail was an effective tool, wasn't it? Though one Luke didn't exactly feel good about.

He told himself he'd only use it as a last resort—assuming, of course, he could create enough emotion in her *to* blackmail. And he was rusty at this wooing business. He needed to get under her skin, find her weakness.

Another wave of guilt washed over him, but, hell, she'd chosen to write the blasted thing, right? She was no innocent in this.

Luke glanced over at Kat, now talking to a customer-service agent. He took in her slim, athletic body, a light sheen of sweat emphasizing the toned muscles of her legs. They reminded him of the colts on his ranch. Kat Callahan had probably been a gangly teenager—all legs—but she'd definitely grown into them since then.

"I'll tell you how you can make it up to me," he said as Kat hung up the phone. She looked at him, confused. "My putting you up for the night," he explained, and he smiled at the instant wariness in her eyes. "When was the last time you went to the top of the Empire State Building?"

Chapter Five

"So?" Luke began as they looked from the observation deck of the Empire State Building out over the forest of steel, concrete, and glass surrounding them that was New York. "When *was* the last time you were up here?"

"When I was a kid," Kat answered, smiling as she remembered, "with my parents and sister." She laughed suddenly, fished around in the bottom of her bag for a moment, and pulled out some coins. Plunking them into a viewer, she swung it around toward SoHo. "I remember my father showed us where we lived." After scanning the low buildings, she finally nodded in satisfaction and pulled away. "There."

Luke looked through the viewer and saw the magnified view of a shabby brick building that had probably once been a warehouse. "Well, it's got character," he said diplomatically.

Kat laughed again. "It did have that. Not much more."

Luke let out a breath at the sight of her brown eyes shining, the sun picking up hints of gold in them. He waited a beat, then asked the question, trying to sound as casual as possible. "So where do they live now, your folks? Not there anymore, I hope."

Kat didn't answer right away but walked farther toward a corner of the observation deck where there were fewer people around. Luke followed.

There was more of a breeze in the corner, and a strand of Kat's hair loosened from her barrette and flew across her lips. She pulled it delicately away and tucked it back behind her ear, a simple but incredibly feminine gesture that stirred something in Luke, something he hadn't felt in a very long time. And something, he realized with surprise, that made him feel instantly guilty, as if he were betraying his beloved Annie.

For a moment Kat stared out at the empty space in the skyline where the World Trade Center towers had once stood so proud and triumphant. Luke also looked at the void. He would never get used to their absence. For years he'd seen them every day, his office just down the block.

Kat suddenly looked at him, her face impassive. "My parents were both killed when I was ten. My sister, Andrea, too."

"Oh, Kat," Luke said, taking a step closer to her, "I'm so sorry." He hoped his voice didn't betray the fact that he'd already known her answer.

But Kat only shrugged lightly. "These things happen."

"But you were so young. That's a lot for a little girl to handle."

Again she shrugged. "These things happen."

Luke suddenly lost patience with her pat answer. "Yes, yes, they happen. I'm sorry it happened to *you*."

Kat glanced up at him, and Luke thought he saw tears glisten. But immediately her jaw set and she swallowed hard.

"So what about you?" she asked, her voice too bright. "What's your story? Did you grow up in Colorado?"

Luke allowed the change of subject. But had he just found her weakness?

"Yep," he answered, forcing a light tone into his voice. "I'm one of the rare natives."

"You mentioned a sister before?"

Luke nodded. "Luanne. She lives in Albuquerque now with her husband."

Oh, what a tangled web we weave immediately ran through his mind, and he couldn't deny the truth of it. He'd try to keep the lies to a minimum, although a few would be unavoidable.

"So how'd you break your nose?" Bright crimson instantly splotched Kat's cheeks as she looked at him, her eyes wide. "Oh, my, that was so rude! I'm so sorry."

"No, that's okay," Luke said, laughing, happy to be able to tell the truth for the moment at least. "I know it's pretty obvious." He fingered the crooked end of his nose. "A newborn foal named Sophie kicked me, her very first act on this planet. My nose rudely got in the way of her perfect little hoof."

"Oh, how cute!"

"Yeah, well," Luke began with a wry grin, "let me tell you, cute *hurts*." He looked at his watch then, knowing more questions were coming. "Well, I don't know about you, but I'm starving."

Kat nodded. "Me too." As they headed inside toward the elevators, she flashed him a smile. "There's something else you need to try while you're here—an authentic New York style pizza—and I know just the place!"

"Lead on," Luke said, hoping she meant Pietro's, his favorite in the whole city.

As the elevator sped down to the ground floor, he stole a glance at her. She was no longer smiling, and he suspected it had something to do with brushing on the subject of her family. Definitely her weakness.

She'd never dealt with her feelings from that terrible time in her life, had she? All that pain trapped inside her, stifling her, blocking her from moving on to any semblance of happiness. He knew exactly how she felt. And he knew also that if she didn't get it out, she'd never move on.

Luke felt suddenly compelled to help this beautiful

but incredibly sad young woman release some of her pain. And just maybe if he *could* help her, he'd feel better about what he was doing.

Half an hour later they were waiting for a large pepperoni and mushroom pizza in the small but bustling Pietro's, complete with red and white checkered tablecloths, the Mets game loud on the TVs, and Pietro himself swirling pizza dough high in the air.

A row of cooks stood behind a glass shield, piling toppings onto pizzas before carefully placing them in the ovens behind them. The place was packed, the only available seating at the counter.

"Isn't this place great?" Kat asked, raising her voice so Tanner could hear her above the din.

He nodded, watching Pietro catch the spinning dough on his plump but incredibly adroit fist.

Finally one of the cooks brought their pizza over, plopping it down on the counter in front of them. "Here you go, folks," he said, whipping out his cutter and swiping it expertly across the pizza, steam rising from each cut. "Enjoy!" he said before rushing back to his place in the assembly line.

"Careful, it's really hot," Kat said, gingerly lifting up one huge flat wedge. She showed Tanner how to fold it in the center and laughed at his expression as she held it up to let some of the grease drip off onto the paper plate. "I like it greasy, but I have my limits!" At last she sank her teeth into the gooey soft mozzarella. A string of it came off with her bite, and she laughed and stretched it out until it broke free.

"So, what do you think?" she asked, smiling. "Is the pizza worth coming two thousand miles for?"

"Definitely," Tanner answered, already halfway through his first piece. "There's nothing like this in Colorado."

Kat took a sip of her soda, then looked at him thoughtfully. "So, what happened to your cowboy act?" Tanner furrowed his eyebrows, not understanding. "I haven't heard a good 'I reckon' or 'y'all' in quite a while."

"Oh," Tanner said, nodding. Was that worry that flickered across his face? But then his lips suddenly parted in a wide grin, and he raised his palms up in a defeated gesture. "Busted. I guess I was just trying to impress you. We don't really talk like that. Some of the men do, especially the ones from Texas or Oklahoma, but not the rest of us for the most part. Coloradoans don't really have an accent. Sorry to disappoint you."

"Believe me," Kat said, laughing as she remembered how much it had irritated her, "I'm not disappointed at all."

"Good," Tanner said around a bite of pizza.

For a moment they ate in silence, absorbing the ambience of the place.

"So," Tanner finally began after a sip of soda, "did it work?"

Now it was Kat's turn to look at Tanner in confusion. "Did what work?"

Tanner leaned in closer to her. "Did I impress you?"

His voice was soft and intimate, and Kat saw with alarm that he was leaning in even closer to her. Her heart hammering in her chest, she saw he was looking intently at her lower lip. Was he going to—Oh, no, he *was*!

"Tanner, I don't think—" she began, mumbling so quietly that there was no way he could hear her in the crowded pizzeria. A second later, though, she started back as she felt the roughness of a cheap paper napkin brushing just beneath her lower lip.

"You had a drop of sauce there," Tanner explained matter-of-factly, but then there was that slow grin curling up his lips as he correctly interpreted her expression. "Why, Miss Callahan," he said, his voice now a soft southern drawl, "whatever did you think I was going to do?"

Kat felt the heat of a blush across the tops of her cheeks. "Never mind," she muttered, dropping a piece of crust onto the grease-stained plate. She looked at her watch. "We should get going. I want to see if Tad called."

Tanner asked for a to-go box, and as they waited for it, Kat frowned, her jaw tight. She hated being so obvious, her emotions right out there in the open. And look how close she'd come to losing it back there when he'd asked about her parents. She never talked about them. *Never.*

Tanner held the leftover pizza box as Kat fished around in her purse for her keys. She could hear the dogs inside the condo, their nails scratching underneath the door. Just as Kat pulled her keys out, Jackie's door swung open.

"Oh, hi there!" she called to them in a singsong voice.

Kat rolled her eyes. Jackie had probably been waiting all afternoon for them, camped out by the peephole in this new outfit. The woman must shop exclusively at secondskin.com. Except for the fringe down the sides, her brown suede pants could have been painted on, they were so tight. And the skimpy hot pink halter top left absolutely nada to the imagination.

"How are you?" Jackie asked, obviously addressing only Tanner.

Kat jammed the key into the lock.

"Just fine, ma'am."

Ma'am? Kat gave Tanner a sharp glance, his cowboy persona suddenly back in full swing. What, was he trying to "impress" Jackie now?

Jackie teetered over to them on her high-heeled boots and lightly touched Tanner on the forearm. " 'Ma'am.' That's so quaint! I just love the way you talk."

Kat let out a breath and held her hand out for the pizza box. "Here, I'll take that in and let you two . . . talk." She couldn't mask the snide undertone in her voice.

Tanner dipped his hat at her and handed her the box. "Mighty obliged, ma'am." Kat was appalled to see him actually wink at her, one side of his mouth curving upward in a knowing smile.

Letting out a breath, Kat opened the door and greeted the dogs, their tails sweeping happily back and forth across the floor, their noses stretching up to smell the leftover pizza. Walking into the kitchen, she shook her head, angry with herself for feeling things she had absolutely no right to feel.

She put the pizza box into the fridge and headed back to the living room. The message light was blinking on the phone console on her desk. She walked over to it and pressed play. The first message was from Brian, wanting an update on the computer situation.

The second was from Tad, asking her to call him back as soon as possible. Kat's stomach tightened at the tone of his voice. She snatched up the phone and dialed his number.

"I'm really sorry," he said right away, "but it didn't work."

"Oh, no," Kat muttered, sitting down heavily.

"I ran the program three times. It's not the program, though, it's your files. The damage was way too extensive. I've never seen anything like it. This virus is just so—"

"I know, I know," Kat said resignedly. "It's just so 'rad.'"

"Fully."

Kat rested her forehead on her palm. She'd known all along that this was a possibility, but she'd refused to believe it might actually happen. She felt as if she'd been punched in the stomach.

"You want me to reinitialize the hard drive?" Tad was asking.

"I don't know what that means," Kat said wearily.

"Wipe it out completely and start from scratch," Tad explained. "It's the only way to totally get rid of the virus."

Ugh. That seemed so final, so irrevocable. Besides,

maybe it was like cryogenics. Maybe one day a future version of that program would be able to recreate her files, especially her novel, *The View from Here.* All those hours—*years*—spent agonizing over each sentence, each word, striving to achieve the perfect vision in her head.

Tears swam in Kat's eyes, and she swallowed hard. "No, thanks," she managed to say. "I'll just come by and pick it up in the morning. Thanks for all your help."

After hanging up she called Brian at Winslow, but he was gone for the day, so she left a voice mail. He'd probably want her to call him on his cell phone, but she simply couldn't face that right now.

Kat no longer heard Tanner and Jackie outside. Either they'd gone inside to Jackie's or they were having an impromptu make-out session right there in the hallway.

Oliver, ever faithful, came over to Kat and sat in front of her, staring up at her adoringly. "Oh, Ollie." Kat burst out into a sudden sob, taking his big chubby head in her hands. She rubbed her face into the thick softness of his fur, her tears clumping together small tufts of his fur.

After letting herself cry out some of her frustration, Kat pulled away from him and wiped her eyes. She didn't have time to wallow in misery. She had to focus on the Janssen book. Still sniffling, Kat opened the third drawer of her desk and pulled out the thick stack of paper.

She was thankful she'd kept the hard copy of the printout with Brian's edits in the drawer, so Lucy hadn't been able to release her destructive force on it.

Taking it over to the couch, she sat down and thumbed through it. It probably wouldn't take her the full four weeks to make the revisions. A lot of that time she'd spent thinking things through, planning out how to incorporate Brian's suggestions and comments, making sure the changes didn't affect anything else in the book. Realistically she was probably looking at two, maybe three weeks.

It occurred to her to take it to Colorado, work on it there, then e-mail it to Brian, but a moment later she realized that Upstairs at Winslow would never risk that. They wouldn't want their potential best seller floating out there on the Internet. Besides, it wouldn't be much of a vacation. She let out another deep sigh, her hands resting on the stack of paper. What to do about Tanner?

As if on cue, he walked in, sans Jackie, thank goodness.

He must have seen it all right there on her face. "What's wrong?"

Kat looked up at him and shrugged forlornly. "It looks as if I'm going to have to delay my trip to the ranch."

"What's wrong?" Tanner asked again, sitting down next to her on the couch and giving her his undivided attention.

"Tad couldn't fix my computer," Kat explained. "The file on it had revisions I'm going to have to do over now. It'll probably take at least a couple of weeks. I'm really sorry. I'm not sure what to do now about . . . our situation."

But Tanner only shrugged. "Well, I don't mind sharing

if you don't. So far you've been a pretty decent room-mate. You don't scratch the furniture or beg at the dinner table. Besides, you're fairly kempt."

Despite everything, Kat couldn't help grinning. " 'Kempt'?"

Tanner shrugged, "Well, you're not *un*kempt."

Kat laughed. She appreciated his cheering her up, es-pecially when he was getting the short end of the stick in this.

"Actually, I think it's a good thing you're staying," Tanner said, reading her mind. He nodded at the dogs, lying nose to nose in front of the TV. "Our dogs are too in love to separate."

"They are, aren't they?" Kat agreed with a fond glance at the dogs.

"Speaking of our masters," Tanner began, standing. "I'll take them out—let you get started on your revi-sions." Heading to the foyer, he called over his shoulder, "Come on, kids, it's walkies time."

Watching Lucy and Oliver jump up and scramble over to Tanner, Kat realized she suddenly couldn't bear the idea of the empty condo, knowing she'd focus on her ru-ined vacation, her lost novel, the problems with the book—both computer-wise and morally—and of course, the *pièce de résistance,* the dreaded anniversary coming up in just two days.

"I'll go with you," she said, rising. "I can't do any-thing anyway until I pick up the old file tomorrow from Winslow."

Chapter Six

The park was teeming with people playing Frisbee,
touch football, Rollerblading, running, biking—everyone
soaking in the warm afternoon sun.

As they strolled through one of the open grassy fields,
a Frisbee sailed overhead. Both Lucy and Oliver took
off after it.

"No!" Tanner and Kat cried out in unison, but it was
too late. The dogs circled around them, their leashes
wrapping around Tanner and Kat's legs, pulling them
together. Laughing, they fell, landing in a tangled heap.
Tanner caught himself just before falling right on top of
Kat, his face hovering mere inches above hers.

His smile faded as he looked into her eyes and then
slowly down to her mouth. Her lips tingled beneath his
gaze. Her breaths were coming quick and shallow, and

for a moment everything seemed to stop, the active scene around them falling away as her heart thudded in her chest.

And then Tanner was lowering his head, closing his eyes, and this time there was no mistaking his intention. And maybe a small part of her wanted it to happen. Still, Kat pressed her fingertips across his lips to stop him.

"No, Tanner," she said, and she barely heard her own voice. His lips were so soft, so impossibly smooth. He opened his eyes, and Kat realized she was still touching his mouth. Quickly she pulled her hand away and sat up.

Lying on his side, Tanner propped his head up on one palm and raised his eyebrows in an unspoken question.

Kat looked over at the dogs, innocently watching the Frisbee fly back and forth. They'd caused this, those monsters. Kat took in a deep breath and let it out slowly. Tanner sat up also and, waiting patiently, unwrapped the leashes from around his ankles.

Kat was having a hard time formulating words. She wasn't sure what she even wanted to say, just that this needed to end here, now. She couldn't handle anything more in her life. She was barely holding on as it was. Maybe in the future she'd be prepared for something more. Just not right now.

"Look, Tanner, I'll admit I find you attractive. It's just that—"

"Well, now," Tanner cut in, his eyes roaming up and down her body as he pretended to assess her, his gaze again settling on her face, a hint of amusement sparkling in the blue of his eyes. "You're not so bad yourself, little lady." *No!* That wasn't fair, springing his whole charming-cowboy thing on her now.

Kat huffed out a breath and looked away from him again, toward the safety of the Frisbee soaring back and forth. This was so awkward. It was easier not to look at him. "*Anyway,*" she began, working hard to instill some sort of resolve into her tone, "this thing that I think we both know is there. Or starting to be there. Whatever." Articulate she was not. He nodded, though, understanding. *Good.*

"It's just not going to work for me. We need to nip it in the bud, right here, right now."

Tanner was silent, and Kat finally glanced at him. He was rubbing a blade of grass between his fingers, apparently mulling over her words.

Kat concentrated on the Frisbee again, but when Tanner still hadn't said anything after another minute, she felt compelled to fill the silence. "So, anyway, don't waste your time on me. I'm sure there are thousands of"—she laughed lightly but heard how hollow it sounded—" 'city girls' around here who would love to—"

"Right now," Tanner gently interrupted, touching the side of her face and turning her to look at him. The amusement was gone from his eyes. "I'm only interested in one city girl. This one." His serious, intent gaze fell to her mouth. He licked his lower lip and leaned toward her. Butterflies suddenly took flight in Kat's stomach. Had she really just met this man *yesterday*?

Yes, she had, and this had to stop. She pulled back abruptly. "Look, I know where this is going, Tanner. The thing is, I don't *do* one-night stands—or week-long ones or even month-long ones for that matter. It's just not in my nature. And that's all this would be, right?"

But he was still gazing at her mouth in that intent way of his. This was not working at all.

"Besides," she said, sitting up straighter and giving him a direct look, her voice now even more resolute, "I'm seeing someone. Brian Winslow, my editor. He's Basil Winslow's grandson."

"Well, good for him." Tanner nodded, that hint of amusement flitting through his blue eyes again, belying the straight, serious line of his mouth. "And is it serious between you two?"

Kat shrugged, aware he was patronizing her but deliberately ignoring it. "It could be," she responded, and not untruthfully. It was completely up to her how serious it became with Brian, and someday she might very well choose to . . . But Tanner was still gazing at her steadily, contemplatively, and she lost her train of thought.

"Well, all right-y, then," Tanner said after a moment, his voice overly cheerful. "I guess that's settled." He stood up and held out a hand to help her up. "Shall we?"

"I'm fine, thanks," Kat said, not taking his hand. She didn't realize, though, that one loop of Lucy's leash was still wrapped around her ankles, and it tripped her up.

With lightning-quick reflexes, Tanner stooped down and caught Kat around her waist, supporting her. Her shirt had come untucked from her shorts, and she was instantly aware of Tanner's fingers against the bare skin at her waist.

As she steadied herself, Kat realized Tanner was stroking that tiny spot of skin with a featherlight touch of his fingertips. She took a step back from him, wishing she could also get away from the eruption of tingles swirling out in all directions from his fingertips.

"Come on, Oliver," she said, tugging a bit too hard on the leash. Briskly leading the way toward the nearest exit from the park, Kat let out a breath, thinking of the next couple of weeks looming ahead. They would be long ones indeed.

They exchanged only a few words on the way home, both deep in their own thoughts. Luke couldn't believe he'd gotten so carried away back there. He'd been a half-second away from kissing her—would have, if Kat hadn't stopped him. And that hadn't been part of his plan. It would have been much too soon.

He'd simply been incapable of stopping himself as he'd gazed down at Kat Callahan's flushed face after they'd fallen, her brown eyes shining, her beautiful mouth opened wide in laughter, looking so eminently *kissable*. She had been breathtaking.

No, don't think that way. This was not about her—the woman. This was about her—the writer. She was the enemy.

Enemy, enemy, enemy.

Maybe if he said the word to himself enough times, he'd come to believe it again. She was just so . . . nice. Somehow she'd gotten under his skin when he wasn't looking. It was supposed to be the other way around!

They were passing the recently closed drugstore, Sav-More, across from Kat's building when she stopped in front of the window. Luke also looked in and saw a coin-operated pony, the only thing left in the store.

"Soon they'll take that away too," Kat said wistfully, her eyes on the old brown pony, the paint on its ears worn away from countless tiny fingers grasping them over the years. "I used to ride him when I was little. I'd come here with my granddad." She glanced at Luke in the reflection in the window. "I stayed with my grandparents after my parents and Andrea . . . you know."

She still had a hard time just saying the word, even after so many years. But he knew what that was like, didn't he?

"My granddad and I would go to the park together when Mrs. Burgstrom came to gossip with my grandmother," Kat was saying. "We'd come here first, and I'd get to ride on the pony. Then we'd go to the soda fountain in the back and buy ice cream cones—a scoop of rocky road for me and a double scoop of mint chocolate chip for my grandfather."

Luke's heart wrenched at the little-girl tone that had crept into Kat's voice as she relived the memory. "We'd eat the cones on the way to the park, talking about anything and everything—except my grandmother. It was like we had our own special ritual that my grandmother couldn't touch."

"He sounds like a wonderful man, Kat," Luke said.

"He was."

"But your grandmother . . . ?"

Kat flashed him a wry smile in the reflection. "Not so much." She let out a long breath before continuing. "She was bedridden the last ten years of her life." With a humorless chuckle she added, "Although I think only the last five were really necessary."

She turned around and leaned against the glass, looking up at the imposing building across the street—her building. Watching her, Luke could almost see the years peel away, her eyes growing dark. "My grandfather loved her very much, though. He waited on her hand and foot. I helped out when I could, but it never seemed like it was enough. My grandmother was very demanding. Nothing was ever good enough for her—not hot enough, cold enough, fast enough. Nothing was ever *enough*."

"Even you?" Luke asked softly, not taking his eyes off her.

"*Especially* me," Kat spat out, turning away from the building to look again at the pony through the window. "Anyway, Mrs. Burgstrom would come visit her, my grandmother, and they'd gossip about everyone in the building." Again Kat let out a mirthless laugh. "It was the only time I really saw my grandmother smile. And even then it was a *mean* one, you know?"

Luke nodded. As he watched her profile, he saw her

jaw ease, her full lips slowly curling up into a smile. He sighed. Yet another turn in the roller-coaster ride that was Kat Callahan.

"Anyway, when Mrs. Burgstrom was there, my grand-father and I would take our walks in the park. I thought of them as our little escapes. My grandfather would never admit it, but I'm sure he did too. I could see how drained he became from her constant need, years spent chasing after her approval—her love maybe, I don't know." She let out a deep sigh. "And then one night five years after I moved in, he went to sleep and never woke up again. I found him."

"Oh, Kat, that must have been so hard."

She nodded, then shrugged matter-of-factly. "After that, until she died when I was eighteen, it was just the two of us. Those weren't good years for me." She'd said the last words so quietly, Luke barely made them out.

With a glance at him, Kat said quickly, "Don't get me wrong. I *did* love her. I mean, she was the only family I had left. But when she died . . ."

"You felt relieved?" Luke suggested after Kat's voice had trailed off. Slowly she nodded. "And guilty for feel-ing that way?"

Kat nodded, tears forming in her eyes. Immediately, though, she frowned as she seemed to suddenly become aware of herself and her surroundings. She stood up straighter and, obviously embarrassed, quickly blinked the tears away as she pulled herself out from the past.

"Oh, why did you let me go on like that? I never do that, and—" She stopped speaking in midsentence as Luke saw her gaze go beyond him, her eyes widening.

Spinning around, she stared hard at the alley across the street, next to her building.

"What is it?" Luke asked, turning to follow her line of sight.

"There was a man there, in a blue jacket," Kat said breathlessly, pointing to the alley. "He ducked into the shadows when he saw me looking at him. I'm pretty sure I saw him a couple of days ago, and he did the same thing. I think he's watching me, Tanner, maybe even following me!"

Luke handed her Lucy's leash. "Stay here," he ordered, and she didn't argue. He half jogged across the street, then walked a few feet into the alley. "There's no one here, Kat!" he called back while furiously gesturing at the bumbling idiot hiding behind the Dumpster to get the hell out of there. At least he'd been on the ball enough to follow Kat to Tad's place—so far, his one saving grace.

Emerging from the alley, Luke gave Kat a wide shrug. She looked so small and scared over there, even with the two big dogs on either side of her. Glancing furtively toward the alley, she crossed the street.

"He probably just lives in the neighborhood," Luke suggested when Kat reached him. He smiled, trying to ease her fear—fear *he'd* caused. "I bet he's got a crush on you, and he's working up the courage to ask you out."

Handing him Lucy's leash, Kat finally grinned. "Or maybe I'm just being paranoid. You're right. He probably does live around here, and that's why he looks familiar. I still think he's creepy, though."

As Kat walked with Oliver toward the building, Luke hung back with Lucy and glanced toward the alley, letting out a frustrated breath. He didn't need any more problems, not now. And his one particular problem with Kat wasn't getting any better—if anything, it was getting worse.

He looked ahead again, seeing her long red curls swinging back and forth airily across her shoulders and upper back. Suddenly a late-afternoon sunbeam cleared a building behind him and shone directly on her.

Luke caught his breath. Her hair seemed to have caught fire, the auburn strands shining—lustrous, radiant, shimmering in a thousand variations of red, every strand a different hue, held in the light for a millisecond, then shifting, ever-changing, like slow-burning embers.

It was the most beautiful thing he'd seen in a long time.

He blinked and looked away from her. "Enemy, enemy, enemy," he muttered, for all the good it did him.

That night, Kat went to bed early, wiped out from pulling her near all-nighter the night before. Still, she lay awake for nearly an hour, her thoughts on the man in the next room.

She couldn't believe she'd told Tanner so much about herself, about her grandfather and her grandmother—

especially her. For years she'd tried very hard to suppress those memories, tried to forget the whiny sound of her voice, the constant sympathy plays, the disapproval in her eyes when Kat didn't say exactly the right soothing words in the appropriate tone of voice in the proper amount of time.

But why had she told all that to Tanner? *Because he seemed to care,* came the immediate answer, and in a way no one had for a very long time, not even Brian.

Even after such a short time it felt as if Tanner could see right through her, his blue eyes penetrating deep beyond the façade she'd worked so hard to maintain through the years. Her defenses fell apart under that intent gaze of his, making Kat feel weak, vulnerable. Yet some part of her wanted him there, welcomed the intrusion into her long-protected psyche.

That was the part she was most afraid of.

Chapter Seven

"**J**ust two weeks, Brian," Kat pleaded, "that's all I'm asking for." But Brian still looked skeptical, his fingers interlaced on top of his desk calendar.

After stopping by Tad's the next morning to grab her doomed laptop, Kat had gone to Brian's office to pick up a flash drive with the last version of the book she'd e-mailed him, the one he'd based his changes on. She needed to get started on the revisions. Brian had told her that Upstairs wanted to get someone else to help with them, but Kat had argued it was important that she do it alone to maintain consistency.

She was actually surprised at how territorial she suddenly felt about it. Maybe it was more about pride. The Janssen book was *hers,* and she'd worked hard on it. She didn't want anyone else messing with her words.

"Besides," she continued in a reasonable tone, "the DNA results aren't in yet, and they have to wait for those, right?"

While Kat had researched and written the book, Winslow had been trying to get DNA samples from all three of the Janssens. They'd even bribed a Beverly Hills trash collector to go through their bags in search of enough material to test. It had been difficult, though. It seemed as if the Janssens knew what was going on and were being extremely careful about what they left in their trash. So far Winslow had gotten their hands on only three usable samples. The first one turned out to be contaminated, and the second one had been lost in a mix-up at the lab. Winslow was now having a third batch tested, but this time, as a precaution, they'd divided the material and were using two different labs.

But Kat didn't like to think about any of that. It all seemed so underhanded and sordid. *And couldn't the book itself be similarly described?* a little voice inside her head whispered, but she pushed that thought away. *A means to an end* had become Kat's mantra to ward off the voice.

Kat realized she was holding her breath as Brian considered what she'd said, his brown eyes thoughtful behind the designer glasses.

At last Brian unclasped his hands and laid them flat on the desk. "All right, you have your two weeks," he agreed, but then he gave her a pointed look. "Understand, though, that as soon as the results are in, Upstairs is going to push for immediate release."

Kat nodded. "I'd better get to it, then." Slipping the flash stick into her purse, she stood up to leave.

Brian also rose and walked around his desk, catching her arm at the door. "Wait," he said, his tone more tender now. As she turned to face him, Kat saw his brown eyes soften. "I know you won't have time to go out during the next couple of weeks, but would you mind if I brought over some take-out a couple of times so we could eat together?"

Kat gave him an apologetic smile. "Thanks, Brian, but I don't think so. I'll probably be working straight through. Any distractions will just delay it."

"Okay," Brian said, his shoulders lowering slightly. "Well, I'll walk you out, then." As they began heading through the maze of cubicles, Kat saw Benny waving to her from across the room, and she waved back.

"Oh, hey," Brian began, "what about the guy from Colorado?"

Why did she feel a sudden pang of guilt at his mentioning Tanner?

"He's already here," Kat told him. "I explained the situation to him, and he said he didn't mind our sharing for a while."

"I bet," Brian scoffed. They'd reached the elevators, and Brian pushed the down button for her. "I'm not sure I like the idea of a strange man living in your condo with you."

"Oh, he's harmless." Harmless in the way Brian meant anyway, Kat thought.

But he was frowning, obviously not reassured by her answer. "Still, though, I know those men get pretty wild out there on those ranches. Lots of drinking too."

"He doesn't exactly fit the stereotype," Kat said with a small laugh. A moment later she realized she was grinning like a schoolgirl with a crush. And Brian must have seen it. His worried frown had deepened into a scowl.

"It'll be fine," Kat said quickly, touching his forearm. "Don't worry."

"All right," Brian said reluctantly as the elevator bell dinged, the doors opening.

Kat stepped in and gave him a bright everything's-fine smile. "See you soon," she said as she doors closed.

Brian smiled back, but it didn't quite reach his eyes.

Kat clicked Save and sat forward in her chair, reaching behind to rub her sore back. She definitely needed a break.

She looked down at the imposing stack of paper on the left side of the laptop and then at the smaller pile on the right—the pages she'd completed. She'd wanted that pile to be a little thicker after an entire day. The revisions were not going as easily or smoothly as she'd thought.

She glanced at her watch. Only a few hours left now. She drew in a long breath, once again forcing her stomach muscles to relax, the dread of the coming anniversary continuing to settle there in a heavy knot of anxiety.

With a surge of warm, clean-smelling air, Tanner came

out of the guest room, his dark curls glistening wet. He put his boots down by the sofa and headed into the kitchen.

An hour or so earlier he'd come in from his day of sightseeing, taken the dogs for a walk, and then gone immediately back into his room, obviously not wanting to disturb her.

What he didn't realize, though, was that he'd been disturbing her all day. She couldn't concentrate, her thoughts relentlessly turning back to him, to their almost-kiss the day before.

More than once Kat had found herself lost in the same vivid daydream, imagining the feel of those soft, strong lips against her own. As she was doing right now, she realized with a start as Tanner walked back into the living room carrying a beer.

She turned to him as he sat down on the sofa and gave him what she hoped was a casual smile. "Hi."

Tanner flashed her a quick grin. "Hi, yourself." He took a sip of beer before rolling up one leg of his jeans to slide his boot on.

"So, what have you been doing all day while I've been slaving away?"

Tanner let out a light chuckle. "Playing Joe Tourist to the hilt: Times Square, Rockefeller Center, the Met." He raised his eyebrows at her, smiling. "See? I'm learning the lingo 'round here. I even know what a 'Lex' is now. Lexington Avenue, right?"

Kat laughed, nodding. "You get an A plus."

With a grunt, Tanner pulled on his left boot, then started rolling up the other side. "And last but not least I took the ferry to see ol' Lady Liberty."

"Wow, that *is* a lot to do in one day. I'm impressed."

"Thanks." Tanner was quiet for a moment as he grabbed his right boot, pulled it on, then unrolled the pant leg back down around it. Finally he took another sip of beer and relaxed back against the couch. "The most exciting part, though, was when a little girl thought she saw Victoria Janssen on the ferry. When everyone scrambled over to that side, I swear we almost capsized!"

Kat sighed, her grin fading. "Well, the Janssens are a pretty hot commodity right now."

"So, where do *you* think they are anyway?"

Kat let out another long breath of air. "Oh, I don't know. Sometimes I think it's all just a big publicity stunt, just in time for the premiere of *T Minus One.* I mean, that's what they do, right? Make movies, get paid obscene amounts of money, then do whatever it takes to get people into the theater?"

"You really think that?"

Kat looked at him, surprised at his tone. "Yes," she said, feeling suddenly defensive for absolutely no reason. Guilt over the book probably. "No," she said quickly without thinking. Oh, she was so tired of this pendulum of emotion when it came to the Janssens. "I don't know."

She suddenly couldn't bear talking about it anymore. Quick change of subject. "So, did you go to Ellis Island too?"

"Nope, it was getting too late. I'll do that another day."

"You really should. It's so interesting. Some of my ancestors came through there from Ireland."

"Really," Tanner said, impressed.

Kat nodded. "McIntyre's Scottish, right? Did any of your relatives come through there?"

Tanner shrugged, fidgeting with the label on his beer. "I'm not sure. My parents never said anything about it." After a moment he nodded over at the laptop. "So how's it going?"

His changing the subject was not lost on Kat. She realized then that Tanner hadn't told her much about himself, even though she'd practically bared her entire soul to him. But that was certainly his prerogative. Maybe she should take a cue from him and adopt that policy herself.

"All right," she answered with a sigh, looking down at the computer but then suddenly shaking her head. "No, actually, it's been completely frustrating. I thought I'd be a lot further along than this." She turned back to him. "You know what? I need a serious break. Do you want to go grab a bite to eat? There's a great Portuguese restaurant a block over, Rafael's. Killer sangria."

With a light chuckle, Tanner took his last sip of beer. "So I've heard. Your neighbor Jacqueline asked ask me to join her there for dinner tonight."

Jacqueline? Kat swallowed a sudden lump in her throat.

"I'm sure she wouldn't mind if you joined us."

"Oh, she'd *love* that," Kat said cattily and immediately regretted it. Thank God she didn't have feathers or they'd be visibly ruffled.

What the heck was she doing? She was the one who'd made it clear the day before where things stood between her and Tanner. What right did she have to get angry if he turned his attentions elsewhere?

"Thanks anyway," she said, trying hard to sound like a grown-up. "I'll just eat the leftover pizza from yesterday. I should probably get back to work anyway." To add credence to her words, she turned back to the laptop, her fingers poised over the keyboard.

"All right-y then," Tanner said. Kat heard the sofa springs creak as he stood and headed back into the kitchen, then heard the clink of the empty beer bottle as he put it into the recycling bin.

As Tanner came back into the living room, Kat looked down studiously at the page she was pretending to work on. In her peripheral vision she saw Tanner go over to Lucy and Oliver, lying in their favorite spot by the TV, and lean down to them.

"Now, you two be good little girls and boys," he said, petting both of them before heading for the door. He paused by Kat's desk. "You're sure you don't want to come along?"

"Yep," she said, with only a quick glance up at him. "Thanks, though." She typed in random words as Tanner strode to the foyer.

"Well, have a good night," he said, opening the door.

This time Kat didn't look up. "You too!" she called, but she immediately winced at how forced her voice had sounded.

She sighed as Tanner closed the door. She'd never been good at deception. How was she ever going to get through the next two weeks?

Chapter Eight

A couple of hours later, Kat looked at her watch and sighed. Tanner and Jackie were probably still at dinner, taking their own sweet time over a pitcher of Rafael's incredible sangria.

Kat could see them perfectly in her mind, tucked away in that cozy booth in the back, playing footsie under the table. Heaven only knew what "Jacqueline" had worn for her grand seduction—

Stop it! Kat banged her fists on either side of the laptop, making it jump. She had to concentrate on her work now. Maybe a glass of wine would help relax her. She headed into the kitchen and grabbed the bottle of Shiraz. There were about two glasses left. She poured herself one and took a long sip.

Walking back into the living room with the bottle,

Kat heard Jackie's shrill laugh out in the hallway and then Tanner's voice, although she couldn't make out the words.

Unable to help herself, Kat went to the door and peered through the peephole. *Just like Jackie had done,* that annoying voice whispered in her head. "Oh, shut up," Kat mumbled, catching sight of Tanner heading toward Jackie's condo.

The sangria had worked its magic, all right. "Well, yippy-dee-doo for them."

Walking back into the living room, she took another long sip of wine. She knew she was drinking too fast—and on an empty stomach—but didn't care. She needed a distraction, didn't want to think about anything at the moment, especially this horrible anniversary. . . .

Deciding the Janssen book could wait, Kat walked up to the fireplace to get closer to the painting hanging over the mantel—her favorite of all her father's paintings, a vivid abstract pulsating with color and energy.

Gazing up at it, she imagined her dad making the brushstrokes, the thoughts and feelings behind each one. Sometimes it worked, and she would sense him right there with her, could almost feel his arm around her shoulder as they both looked up at his painting. But it was a tenuous, fragile connection that never lasted and tonight didn't come at all. It felt just out of her reach, teasing her, mocking her.

The colors blurred together as tears filled Kat's eyes. She blinked hard, turned away from the painting, and collapsed onto the couch. She poured the rest of the Shiraz into her glass, switched on the TV, and channel-surfed for a while as she drank the wine, welcoming the increasing haze. It was so much easier now to brush away unpleasant thoughts. If only she could *always* feel this way.

She looked over at the dogs, nestled together in a corner. "Hey, y'all, come on over here," she called to them. "I reckon I'd like to pet you right about now."

Happy for the attention, the dogs jumped up and scurried to Kat, plopping down on either side of her, their tails thwapping against the floor.

Kat slid down off the couch and wrapped an arm around each dog. "I love you guys *so* much. *You* love me, right?" She was answered by a lick on the cheek from Oliver and a nudge on the arm from Lucy's wet nose. "At least somebody does," Kat mumbled, aware she was in the midst of a serious pity party. But for one night she was going to allow herself some good old-fashioned wallowing.

Reaching for her glass, she swallowed the last of the wine just as the front door opened. In walked Tanner McIntyre, fresh from his hot date.

"Well, howdy, pardner!" Kat called with a sloppy wave.

"Hi," Tanner said, giving her a hesitant smile. "Why are you on the floor—" His eyes widened when he saw the empty Shiraz bottle on the coffee table. "Did you drink the rest of that?"

Kat's shoulders stiffened defensively. "It was only two glasses."

Tanner raised his eyebrows. "Dollars to donuts you didn't eat anything beforehand."

"I had a pretzel." Hours ago. "But never mind me." She heaved herself back up onto the couch and patted the cushion beside her. "Come, sit. I want to hear all about your big date!"

Tanner flashed her a dubious glance. "Really."

Kat nodded. "Absolu-ly."

"I'm not sure that's a word, but okay." Tanner gave in, sitting down beside her but leaving a lot of breathing room.

Kat knew he was only humoring her, but she was glad he'd sat down anyway. "So, tell me," she began, reaching over to give him a maternal pat on the leg, "how was it?"

Tanner chuckled. "Just fine. Rafael's was great, as promised and—"

"Yeah, yeah," Kat cut in, waving a hand dismissively. "Cut to the good stuff." Leaning close to him again, she asked in a conspiratorial whisper, "Did you kiss her?"

"And then we got some ice cream," Tanner continued, ignoring her question.

No way was she letting that happen. "Come on, tell me."

"Then we came back to her place. . . ."

"Yeah, and . . . ?"

"Well, we were sitting on her couch, just talking, then she leaned in real close. Kind of like this." He leaned in closer to Kat, and she breathed in the musky, natural scent of him. "Then she tucked some of my hair back, kind of like this."

Taking a strand of Kat's hair, Tanner gently pushed it back behind her ear. Closing her eyes, Kat leaned forward, savoring his touch.

"Then she . . ." Tanner began again, and Kat thought she heard a husky new edge to the words.

"Mmm?" Kat murmured.

"Then she fell asleep!" Tanner let out a raucous laugh. "Too much sangria, I suppose."

Kat's shoulders sagged, and she opened her eyes. Undeniably she was glad that nothing had happened between them, but at the same time she felt vaguely dissatisfied.

Tanner leaned forward again and picked up the empty Shiraz bottle. Tipping it back and forth, he shook his head. "Boy, you city girls sure can drink!"

"Well, it just so happens that I had a reason!" Kat declared.

She scooted over on the couch away from him as the reason—*reasons*—flooded painfully back over her. Fighting tears, she looked down at her hands and rubbed her thumbs together.

After a moment Tanner leaned over and drew back the curtain of hair that had been hiding Kat's face. Glancing at him, Kat saw a combination of amusement and genuine concern in his eyes. Kat stared back down at her hands, humiliation settling over her like a hot, scratchy blanket.

"Well now," Tanner began, his tone soft, understanding. "I'm not vain enough to think this is *all* because of me."

Kat gave him a sharp look, not at all liking his smug assumption, but his voice had been so gentle, his questioning eyes so tender, she didn't call him on it.

"What time is it?" she asked after a long moment.

Tanner looked at his watch. "Five after midnight."

Kat let out a shaky breath. "Well, at exactly 2:37 A.M. I'll be thirty years old."

"Really," Tanner said, sitting back on the sofa in surprise. "Well, happy birthday."

"Thanks," Kat mumbled, playing with her thumbs again.

"Not happy about it, I take it?" Tanner asked.

Fresh tears welled in Kat's eyes, and this time she was powerless to stop them. Tanner reached over to the tissue box on the side table and pulled one out for her.

As Tanner waited patiently, Kat wiped her eyes and blew her nose. Blinking away more tears, she finally began. "Twenty years ago today, on my tenth birthday, my parents and sister Andrea were on their way to pick me up from school. We were going to the Bronx Zoo and then out to dinner. It was supposed to be my special d-day."

Kat's voice broke on the last word, and she had to swallow hard before continuing. "They never made it. A semi came around a corner too fast, and—" The next words caught in her throat, and she couldn't continue.

"Oh, Kat," Tanner said, moving over to put his arm around her shoulders. "I'm so sorry. And on your birthday." He handed her another tissue as tears coursed down her cheeks.

When she was able to speak again, Kat continued. "That's why I wanted to go to Colorado—as a distraction, I guess." She smiled at him through her blurry vision. "For weeks I've been focusing on this image—me, lying in a meadow, the sun warm on my face, the smell of wildflowers everywhere." She closed her eyes, picturing it again. "Only the birds and maybe a stream nearby breaking the absolute quiet."

Right on cue, a sustained honk blared up from the street below. Kat drew in a breath and let it out in a rush of irritation. "It's always so noisy here! You're constantly aware of people around you. *So* many people."

"I thought you liked the city."

"Oh, I do," Kat said quickly with a glance at him before looking back down at her hands. "It's . . . familiar to me."

"Safe?" Tanner suggested in his gentle way, but this time it only sent a spike of unreasonable anger through Kat. No longer in the mood for his condescension, she moved out from under his arm.

"Fine, you win," she barked. "It's *safe*. Happy now?"

"Oh, dang it, Kat, I'm sorry," Tanner said, self-anger clear in his voice. "I didn't mean to upset you even more."

"It's okay," Kat mumbled.

"But about the ranch," Tanner began, "you'll still

have all that, just delayed a little. And it'll be even better than you think, I promise. You forgot about the mountains surrounding that meadow of yours, rising up all around you, huge and still and timeless. They're spectacular, especially at night. They look like ghosts, the snow on the peaks almost glowing in the moonlight. And the stars . . . You're going to love it."

Kat nodded but felt the tears coming again. Instead of making her feel better, his words had only depressed her further, reminding her of all she was missing.

"Come on," Tanner said, rising. "Let's get you to bed. You'll feel better in the morning." He leaned down to wrap his arm around her waist.

"G-gallop," Kat mumbled through her tears.

Tanner sat back down next to her, the amused smile once again curling his lips. "What?"

"I wanted to gallop," Kat repeated.

"I thought that's what you said."

"When I was little," she explained, "my parents took me to the SoHo street fair. There was a horse, a Clydesdale, named Charlie." She stood up and went to the mantel above the fireplace where she kept her framed photos. She picked up the one in the blue frame and brought it over to him.

"That's me and Charlie," she continued, handing him the picture. It showed her at five, looking impossibly small atop an enormous brown horse, her bright red pigtails blazing in the sun. She wasn't smiling. Instead, her lower lip jutted out in a frustrated pout.

"The man led the horse around in a slow, wide circle." She laughed. "*Slow.* I couldn't stand it."

Tanner smiled in amused understanding. "You wanted to gallop."

"Yep," Kat said, still looking at the picture as Tanner placed it on the coffee table in front of them. "I even kicked him in the sides to make him go fast, but old Charlie was having none of that." Tanner chuckled. "By the time I got off him, I was in full tantrum mode. My parents promised they'd take me galloping when I was older—probably just to shut me up."

Her smile faded as she continued, "My grandfather told me a couple years later that my parents had planned a surprise for me on my tenth birthday. We weren't going to the zoo after all but to a farm on Long Island, where I was going to get my first riding lesson so I could learn to gallop."

She let out a deep breath. "Afterward, he—my grandfather—always meant to take me, but my grandmother . . . Well, I never did get to gallop."

"You're definitely going to the right place for galloping," Tanner said in an obvious effort to cheer her up. "We have some great horses on the ranch. There's one, Pepperjack, I think you'll really love. He's gentle and understanding with new riders. And an ace galloper . . ."

But Kat was crying again. "It's not just that, though—galloping or my parents or even the revisions. There's something else." She drew in a shaky breath. "On the laptop, there was another file. It was m-my . . ." She choked on a sudden sob and shook her head, unable to continue.

Oh, how she yearned for the haze of the wine, but it had worn off, leaving her defenseless to all of it—the loneliness, the grief, her lost dream. It was too much. Kat lowered her face into her hands, her shoulders quaking as uncontrollable sobs wracked her entire body.

"Oh, come 'ere," Tanner said, drawing her into his arms and rocking her gently. "It's okay," he murmured, "get it out. Get it all out. I'm sorry you're hurting so much."

Kat didn't know how long he held her there, soothing her with his calm, sweet sympathy. Never before had she let herself go like this with another person. Ever. It must have been the culmination of so many terrible events. It was kind of understandable, right?

Slowly, the acuteness of her misery abated, although a solid core of it remained. She was used to that, though. It was the unexpected attacks she had a hard time with.

As the tears finally slowed, Kat became more aware of Tanner. She closed her eyes and breathed in the fresh, clean-laundry scent of his shirt. She nuzzled her face against the smooth side of his neck, his curls brushing against her cheek like the tips of feathers.

Kat's left hand lay against the pocket of his shirt, and she became aware of his heart beating underneath it. Was it speeding up? She pressed a little harder and was sure. The beats were coming faster now—as hers undoubtedly were.

She moved her head slightly, just enough to brush her lips across the warm thickness of his neck. Kat heard, *felt,* him let out a breath. She moved her hand across his chest, the muscles under there tensing beneath her touch.

But then he was laying his hand over hers, gently pulling it off. "Enough," he said in a soft, husky voice. He gathered her up into his arms and rose effortlessly.

Luke kicked the door of her room open, walked inside, and set Kat carefully down on the bed. "Well," he said, rising, "I guess I'll say good—"

But Kat had reached up to him, wrapped her arms around his neck, and was now pulling him toward her.

It took every ounce of strength Luke had to gently disengage her arms and lean back away from her.

She looked up at him in confusion. "I thought you wanted to kiss me."

Luke swallowed hard. "What I *want* is for you to go to sleep and feel better about everything in the morning."

Kat searched his eyes for a moment; then Luke saw anger flick through them.

"Fine," she huffed, and she plopped down on her side, facing the wall. She yanked the covers up haphazardly.

For a long moment Luke just watched her, unable to drag himself away. After a minute her shoulders began to rise and fall steadily, her breaths evening as she fell deeper into sleep. More than anything in the world Luke wanted to lie down beside her and cradle her in his arms as she slept.

He wanted to hold her, protect her, even from herself.

He wanted to free her from the stifling emotional cage he knew so well.

Luke raked a hand through his hair. This was all so unexpected and quickly beginning to reel out of control. Beginning to? Heck, it was a done deal. Any power he'd hoped to gain over her was gone. She had all the power now.

Overcome with the need to see her face before he went back to his own room, Luke walked around to the other side of the bed and gazed down at her. He had to suppress a sudden laugh when he saw that she'd fallen asleep pouting, her lower lip jutting out, her eyebrows still furrowed.

It reminded him of the five-year-old Kat he'd seen in the photo. Fondly he leaned over and kissed her cheek and brought the covers up farther, tucking them in around her.

Yes, he thought, turning off the light and closing her door, this tough cookie was a little undercooked, all doughy and warm in the center. He wanted to see more of that. He sighed as his purpose here came back to him like the cold shower he should probably take right about now.

Maybe he should just come clean with her, tell her the truth about everything. But a second later he imagined her face once she knew, could vividly see, *feel,* the fury in her eyes once she learned how he'd deceived her, worming his way into her life.

What the hell was he going to do?

Chapter Nine

"Well, happy flippin' birthday to me," Kat grumbled the next morning, closing the screen of the laptop a little too hard. If one more thing went wrong . . .

She'd just sat down to work. Tanner must have been out with the dogs for what Kat hoped would be a very long walk. She didn't need to see him right now after what happened last night. It all kept repeating in her mind—kissing his neck, grabbing him in her bedroom, begging to be kissed. Where was the *Undo* button when you needed it?

Letting out a rush of air, Kat looked down at the still-too-thick pile of revisions to be made. On the page she was on now, Brian had scrawled *Year?* in the margin next to a mention of Alex Janssen's first Academy Award nomination.

She'd forgotten how many small things she'd had to look up during the first go-round of revisions, and of course she hadn't saved or printed out any of the information. That would have made it too easy!

But when Kat had tried to look up Alex Janssen's first Oscar nomination on the Internet, she found that her connection had slowed to a snail's pace. It had worked fine the day before, but now it took almost a full minute for each new page to load.

Enough of this. She'd go into Winslow and get Benny to fix her slow connection. While he did that, she'd find a quiet office somewhere and get to work. It would be easier to concentrate there anyway.

And, she thought, getting up quickly, almost toppling over her chair, if she left right now, she could put off the humiliation of seeing Tanner that much longer.

Grabbing the stack of paper and her laptop, she hurried to the foyer. Her hopes for a quick getaway were instantly dashed when she heard Lucy and Oliver scuffling outside the door.

"Figures," she muttered, opening the door for Tanner and the dogs.

"Well, good morning," he said cheerfully, holding up a paper bag with an Elmo's logo on it. "A birthday bagel just for you!"

"Thanks," Kat mumbled, barely looking at him as she took the bag, willing her face to change back to its normal color instead of the red splotches she felt hot on her cheeks. Tanner unleashed the dogs and then sat down on the couch, snapping open the paper.

Now was the time. She'd rehearsed a little speech earlier while lying in bed listening for him to leave with the dogs.

Summoning her courage, Kat put down her things and walked back into the living room. She stopped in front of Tanner, her hands on her hips. "Look, Tanner," she began, but she stopped when he only raised his eyebrows expectantly, his eyes scanning the front page.

"Uh-huh?" he said distractedly.

"Please, Tanner, I have something I need to say." Kat made her voice firm.

"Oh, sorry," Tanner said, folding up the paper and crossing his arms, giving her his full attention.

Kat took in a deep breath and then began reciting her lines. "I apologize for this situation, and if I could give you a refund or something, I would. I also apologize for . . . last night."

She hesitated, flustered as the embarrassing images once again paraded through her mind. Taking in a resolute breath, she continued. "I know my behavior at the end there ran counter to what I'd said to you in the park, but obviously I was upset. Now, though, I want to reiterate that I need us to remain strictly roommates."

There. Message delivered. Again. With luck, it would take this time. For her too.

As before, Tanner seemed to contemplate her words

for a moment before slowly nodding. "I understand," he said solemnly, his features rigid and serious. Too serious, Kat realized. He was only humoring her again!

Exasperated, Kat let her arms fall to her sides. "*Do* you?" she asked pointedly, cocking her head.

Tanner seemed to realize his mistake then, and his expression softened, sincerity filling his eyes. "Okay, yes, I do, Kat. I get it. Strictly roommates."

"Good," Kat said decisively. It was enough for now. Besides, she had to get going. "I'll be at Winslow all day, so you can have the place to yourself." She walked back to the foyer to get her things. She grabbed the Elmo's bag and waved it at him. "Thanks again for the bagel."

Closing the door behind her, Kat leaned against it and let out a breath of relief, glad to be away. It might actually not be a bad idea to keep working at Winslow from now on.

That way she'd only have to get through the nights with him.

Inside the condo, Luke lowered the paper, shaking his head in self-reproach. He hadn't thought she'd go to the Winslow building to do her research. What happened to the good old-fashioned library? Now she'd be spending the whole day with that Brian Winslow character. If he'd known that, he never would have reconfigured her Internet connection.

"No!" Luke slammed his fists down into the paper, making wrinkly dents in it. *That* had been part of the plan—anything he could do to cause a delay. Only a few days before he'd been so focused, his mind on only one thing. And now . . . How could he possibly continue this charade?

Raking his fingers through his hair, Luke forced himself to remember why he was doing this and felt his resolve surge reassuringly back to him. He *had* to do it. There was no one else.

Luke smiled as the idea came to him. A little distraction would certainly fit in with the plan.

"Dang it all," Kat mumbled, jiggling her key up and down in the lock at the front door of her building. It wouldn't budge. After a long day at Winslow huddled in a tiny cubicle, all she wanted to do was get inside and relax, although that would be extremely difficult if Tanner were there.

Kat had fought her thoughts and feelings about him all day despite the dozens of city blocks separating them. It was ridiculous. She'd only known the man a couple of days. How could he have affected her so deeply so fast?

"Here, let me try." Kat turned to see Mrs. Burgstrom standing behind her, back from her evening walk with Walton.

"Thanks," Kat said, pulling her key out and stepping aside as Mrs. Burgstrom inserted her key. Of course, it turned the lock as smoothly as if the blasted thing were coated with WD-40.

"How are you?" Kat asked politely as Mrs. Burgstrom opened the door.

"Fine," Mrs. Burgstrom answered with a curt nod. Following her through the lobby, Kat smiled wryly to herself. Apparently, she was back to *persona non grata* status, no longer riding on the coattails of Tanner's charm.

They rode up the elevator in silence, which was fine with Kat. She needed to concentrate on relaxing, her heart beating faster with each passing floor, her stomach already swarming with butterflies, all in anticipation of seeing Tanner McIntyre. What, was she back in high school?

She couldn't help but compare it to the way she felt— or—*didn't* feel—about Brian. There was none of that with him, not one butterfly, not even a moth.

Brian. Kat didn't know what to do about him. After finding her a cubicle to work in, he'd left her alone for the most part but had stopped by a couple of times to see if she needed anything. He'd also brought her back a turkey wrap for lunch.

Sooner or later she'd have to come right out and tell him she wasn't interested in anything long-term with him. It was hard, though, because there *was* no real reason. Brian was a "great guy"—attractive, considerate, affectionate. He'd make someone a wonderful husband, just not Kat Callahan.

She'd been sensing lately, though, that was the direction he wanted to take. She could see it in his eyes when he looked at her. It wasn't fair to him to continue without saying anything.

Yes, Kat thought with a decisive nod as she followed Mrs. Burgstrom off the elevator and walked toward her condo, she'd aim for *sooner.* Besides, if and when she *was* ready for something more, she wanted someone who set at least a couple of butterflies loose in her stomach, just not the mass migration currently taking place in there and worsening with each step.

It turned out she didn't have to worry. Tanner wasn't home. Only Oliver and Lucy were there to greet her when she opened the door.

"Hi, guys," Kat said, bending down to pet them. They didn't seem as ravenously hungry as usual. Tanner must have fed them and then gone out again. With his new pal "Jacqueline" perhaps?

Kat forced herself to relax her jaw. What right did she have to be annoyed at that?

Shaking her head, she went into the kitchen to order some food. Chinese maybe. Wang's sesame chicken might be good—

But then Kat saw on the front of the refrigerator, amid the brightly colored take-out menus, a piece of notebook paper: *You are cordially invited to join your new roommate and assorted deer and antelope currently playing up on the range (previously known as the roof). P.S. No discouraging words allowed.*

Kat laughed, her heart swelling with happiness despite her earlier resolve. A breeze ruffled the menus, and she looked over to see that the kitchen window was open. Outside was the fire escape leading up to the rooftop deck.

Kat unclipped the barrette at the nape of her neck and shook her hair loose, then bent down to check her reflection in the metal toaster. *No!* she scolded herself, straightening. *He's only your roommate.* "Roommate, roommate, roommate."

Still, though, she couldn't help smiling from ear to ear as she climbed out onto the fire escape.

Chapter Ten

Kat heard them before she reached the top of the fire escape. Coyotes! Apparently a band of them had gathered on the rooftop of her co-op while she was out.

Her heart racing—and not just because of the exertion of the two flights of steps—Kat stepped out onto the roof—or *the range,* as Tanner had called it.

He was alone on the roof, his back to her as he tended the grill all the tenants shared. In front of the grill lay a thick plaid blanket, bouquets of wildflowers at each corner. A portable CD player next to the blanket filled the air with the sounds of a western night—the coyotes, a field full of crickets, the occasional hooting of an owl, even a distant gurgling stream complete with a bullfrog or two.

Kat burst out into a laugh of absolute delight. Tanner

turned to her, smiling and raising his arms, barbecue tongs in one hand. "So?" he called to her. "What do you think?"

"I think it's wonderful!" Kat gushed, walking toward him. As she got closer, she sniffed the air a couple of times. Along with the wildflowers, she smelled something odd in the smoke billowing from the grill.

Walking up to it, she looked inside, curious. Instead of the charcoal briquettes she expected to see, pieces of wood burned in a pile, the embers at the bottom glowing bright orange and yellow.

"Mesquite," he explained. "I had a heck of a time finding it."

"Ah," Kat said, nodding.

"And forget a good steak sauce," Tanner scoffed. "I ended up making it myself." He nodded down at a bowl next to the grill filled with a rich-looking reddish brown sauce.

Kat laughed. "Actually, I think Sparks or Keens would take issue with you on that point."

Tanner grinned. "Hey, if they can't take the heat . . ."

Beside the bowl sat two sirloin steaks so huge, the meat hung over the rim of the plate. Next to it two vegetable kebobs rested on a paper towel—plump cherry tomatoes, mushrooms, and thick chunks of squash squeezed tightly on the skewers.

"I already started the potatoes," Tanner told her, pointing the tongs at two foil-covered shapes nestled in the embers. "They take a long time."

Kat shook her head in wonder at it all. "Wow," was all she could think of to say.

Tanner smiled and gave Kat a light shrug as he picked up one of the steaks with the tongs. "I figured if the lady can't make it to the West, bring the West to the lady." He placed the steak carefully on the grill and picked up the other one.

"Well, thanks. What a nice surprise." Unexpectedly, tears welled in Kat's eyes. Embarrassed, she blinked them away and looked down at the grill, the second steak sizzling as it hit the metal, flames licking at the meat.

Thankfully, Tanner didn't notice her tears, busying himself with placing the kebobs on the grill. It was a tight squeeze. "Go, sit, relax. There's sodas in there." He nudged a cooler sitting beside the grill with his foot.

"You thought of everything, didn't you?" Kat said, bending down to the cooler. She tugged up the top of it and grabbed a couple of Cokes, handing one to Tanner.

Cracking open the ice-cold soda, she sat down on the blanket, took a sip, then put the can down next to her. She lay back on the blanket, crossing her arms above her head, gazing up at the deepening blue of the sky.

Tanner chuckled softly. "I'm sorry you can't see the stars better. It's a lot different on the ranch, far away from any city lights. There you can see the entire night sky splayed out above you. I tried, though. I went around your condo turning on all the lights, hoping to start a city-wide blackout, but the dang grid held."

Kat laughed. "It's okay. I'll suffer." She closed her

eyes, listening to the night sounds from the CD player, the sizzling of the steaks, and the crackling fire. She inhaled deeply through her nose and took in the tantalizing aroma of cooking meat and the scent of the wildflowers surrounding her, pungent and bittersweet.

In fact, except for the continual low rumble of traffic and an occasional honk, she found she really could project herself from the middle of Manhattan straight into that western meadow she'd been so longing for.

"You should patent this stuff," Kat told Tanner, savoring the last piece of sauce-drenched sirloin. He'd cooked it exactly as she liked, slightly charred on the outside, tender and pink in the center.

The mesquite flavor perfectly complemented the tangy homemade steak sauce. The entire meal had been wonderful, the potatoes fluffy and moist from cooking in the foil, the vegetables subtly spiced with thyme and fresh pepper.

"I'm glad you liked it," Tanner said, taking her plate as he stood up. He put the plates into the box he'd brought everything up in, then headed for the fire escape. "I'll be right back," he said over his shoulder.

While Tanner was gone, Kat gathered up the utensils and spices and added them to the box. She chuckled softly to herself. "Stop smiling, you. You're going to break something!"

A few minutes later Kat turned to see Tanner walking

across the roof with two rocky-road ice cream cones, one with a lit candle sticking out of the top.

Kat laughed. "You remembered!"

"Of course. Now hush." As he walked across the rooftop, he sang "Happy Birthday to you" in a passable tenor. On the last note, he dramatically held out her cone. "Now make a wish."

But Kat shook her head. "I can't think of anything to top this." Actually she could, even though she knew it couldn't happen. But that's why they called it a wish, right? Closing her eyes, she leaned forward and blew out the candle.

They sat back down on the blanket and enjoyed their cones in a comfortable silence.

"So," Tanner finally began, "I've been meaning to ask, what's your book about anyway?"

Kat let out a breath, her smile fading. "The Janssens—Alex, Victoria, and Jeremy."

"Like a biography?" Tanner asked, cocking his head to catch a stray drip running down his cone.

"Kind of," Kat said, thinking about how much to tell him. *What could it hurt?* she decided. Tanner didn't seem like the type to go running to *Juicy Weekly*'s competitors to sell a hot story. "Well, you know how they're always in the papers and on TV purporting to be the perfect, normal family?"

Kat had meant the question to be rhetorical, but Tanner was shaking his head. "I don't know, it doesn't seem to me like it's on purpose. I mean, aren't most of those shots taken by the paparazzi on the sly? And I think I remember hearing that Victoria Janssen got out of the business expressly to concentrate on being a 'normal' mother."

"But what about *Alex* Janssen?" Kat countered. "He has two movies coming out next month, one of which made him the highest paid actor *ever*." But that wasn't the point. "Stars use the media when it's convenient for them, promoting their movies and themselves, but then they get upset when the tables are turned on them."

Uh-oh. Had she turned into Brian in the last few minutes? But maybe making his argument would help her actually believe it. "The way I see it, that's the price they pay. They *chose* that life after all. They *wanted* to be famous."

"Did they?" Tanner shrugged. "Maybe they just wanted to act."

"Well, they should have stuck to community theater then," Kat ended in a huff, crunching down on the rim of her cone, fully aware of how defensive she sounded.

"I'm sorry, Kat," Tanner said softly after a moment. "I didn't mean to get you all riled up on your birthday."

"It's okay," Kat muttered.

"So anyway," Tanner began, his tone lighter now, "you were going to tell me about your book."

But Kat didn't want to talk about the Janssens anymore. "Let's just say it's going to make a huge splash when it comes out," she said by way of closing off the topic.

In her peripheral vision, Kat could see Tanner look at her for a long moment before shrugging. "Okay, I get it. Double top secret. I guess I'll just have to wait with the rest of the world."

He popped the last bite of his cone into his mouth and laid down on the blanket. Kat finished her cone too and laid down next to him, keeping a foot or so of space between them. They both gazed up at the stars, more visible now against the blue-black night sky.

"So," Tanner began after a few minutes, "did you always want to be a writer?"

"Uh-huh," Kat answered. "When my parents read to me when I was little, I'd make up different endings to all the stories. And then in elementary school I started writing my own silly little stories. My dad illustrated them. He was an artist."

"Really," Tanner said.

With a wry chuckle, Kat explained, "Never a very successful one, though. He had a couple of solo shows and got pretty good reviews, but he didn't sell many pieces." She laughed again. "Remember that apartment house I showed you from the Empire State Building?" Tanner nodded. "We lived in the tiniest apartment in the building, the four of us. My dad always had paintings drying around the house. It was a little . . . tight." She smiled fondly at the memory. "I can't tell you how many shirts I ruined brushing up against them. My dad didn't mind, though, the smudges I made on his paintings. He said they added a little extra something to them."

"Are those his paintings hanging downstairs?" Tanner asked. Kat nodded, feeling oddly touched that he'd noticed them. She herself had memorized them. Still, something new always seemed to jump out at her—a shade of blue she hadn't noticed before or a subtle highlight that added a whole new dimension to the piece.

"I think they're great," Tanner said. "Very Pollack-y, if that's a word."

Kat nodded, smiling. "My dad worshipped him."

"And you worshipped your dad, didn't you?" Tanner asked in his gentle, searching way.

And suddenly, Kat was crying again. She sat up, laughing a little as she grabbed the napkin that had been wrapped around her cone and wiped under her eyes with it. "I swear I haven't cried in the last ten years as much as I have in the last two days."

Tanner smiled, but there was concern in his eyes. "I'm sorry if I upset you again."

"No, you didn't," Kat insisted, sniffling. "You just seem to have a knack for getting stuff out of me—stuff I usually keep pretty well under wraps."

"Sorry," Tanner said again with a sheepish shrug.

Kat took in a long, ragged breath. "Don't be. It's probably a good thing."

"Okay, but enough of this sad-sack business. Back to our regularly scheduled birthday." He jumped up, holding out a hand to her. "I've got one more thing planned."

"What is it?" Kat asked, still cautious, but she took his hand.

"It's a surprise," Tanner answered, helping her up. "Come on, help me get some of this stuff downstairs."

They took the CD player, the cooler, and the box of dirty dishes down to the kitchen.

"I'll get the rest later," Tanner said, heading for the front door.

"Really, where are we going?" Kat asked, smiling a little hesitantly.

"I told you," Tanner answered sternly, "it's a surprise."

He ducked into his room and brought out a backpack.

"What's in the bag?" Kat asked, curious.

"Hey," Tanner said, looking at her with mock severity. "Exactly what part of 'surprise' do you not get? Now shush." He grabbed her hand and led her to the front door. "Sorry, kids," he called over to Lucy and Oliver, who had raised their heads in unison, hoping for a walk. "Just the adults this time." Pulling a red bandana out of his back pocket, he turned back to Kat. "Okay, now turn around."

"No way," Kat said, laughing when she saw him folding the bandana to blindfold her.

"Oh, come on," Tanner said, taking a step closer and looking down into her eyes. "Or don't you trust me?" he challenged, raising an eyebrow. But as she watched, the amusement faded from his eyes, replaced by a tender softness that made Kat's heartbeat quicken.

"I trust you," she murmured, turning around quickly so he wouldn't see her reddening cheeks. She closed her eyes, silently repeating her new mantra, *roommate, roommate, roommate,* in her head.

Tanner covered her eyes with the bandana, tying the knot in the back gently but securely, careful not to pull her hair. "Done," he declared, and he steered her to the door.

Chapter Eleven

Once downstairs, he led her through the lobby. Thankfully, Kat didn't hear anyone around. But there'd definitely be people outside on the street.

"Everyone's going to think you're kidnapping me or something," Kat whispered.

"With that smile? I don't think so. Besides, this is New York City. You can get away with anything here—or so I've heard."

He opened the front door and walked her down the steps, then stopped her once they'd reached the sidewalk.

"Ever play Pin the Tail on the Donkey?" he asked.

"Sure," Kat answered, feeling very self-conscious, aware that people were probably staring at them.

"Good, then you know the drill."

Kat groaned as Tanner began spinning her around.

After the fifth time, a wave of dizziness almost made her fall down.

"I guess that'll do," Tanner said, steadying her, then taking her elbow and leading her up the street. Or down? Kat didn't know. The old trick had worked perfectly, completely disorienting her.

Kat laughed nervously, trying to be a good sport, and heard a couple of people behind her also laughing as they speculated about what Tanner and she were doing. Kat sensed, though, that they weren't laughing *at* her, more *with* her. Suddenly she didn't feel ridiculous or self-conscious anymore but as if she were a part of something fun and exciting. Her shoulders relaxed, and she smiled more genuinely, letting herself enjoy Tanner's game.

"Okay," Tanner said, stopping her. "Here's a curb. Step down." She did, and a few seconds later he walked her up the curb on the other side. So they'd crossed a street. He spun her around three more times, then walked her a few feet farther before turning her left and crossing another street.

Finally he stopped. "We're here. Now stay."

Kat heard what sounded like a dial spinning, followed by a metallic creak and then the jangling of keys. A moment later came the sound of a lock turning and then the swish of a heavy door opening. A rush of cool air swept over her.

"Okay, come on in," Tanner invited, taking her arm again. As they walked a few steps forward, Kat heard the echo of their shoes against a linoleum floor.

"I'll be right back," Tanner said, moving away, and then Kat heard the click of a switch and the hum of fluorescent lights flickering on. "All right, we're almost there." He led her a few more feet and stopped. A coin jingled down a metal slot, followed by a low rumbling and a loud whirring. And then she knew.

Bursting out into a laugh, she lifted her hands to swipe off the blindfold. They were in the closed Sav-More, right across the street from her building! The familiar sounds she'd heard came from the old pony ride starting up. Kat pushed Tanner playfully. "Oh, you."

"Hey," he said, raising his arms defensively, "you were the one who wanted to gallop! This was the best I could do on short notice. Now come on and mount your trusty steed." He nodded toward the window. "Your audience awaits."

Audience? Frowning, Kat looked beyond the ride and out the window. A crowd of fifteen or so people stood out there, looking inside and smiling. They must have hung around to find out what Tanner was up to as he paraded Kat blindly up and down the street.

"Get on!" she heard a couple of them say even through the window glass.

"Great," Kat mumbled good-naturedly as she climbed up onto the pony. "The one time New Yorkers get involved, and it's to help humiliate the heck out of me."

The springs of the ride groaned under her weight, but the pony diligently moved back and forth beneath her, the undulating motion as familiar to Kat as if she'd ridden it just yesterday. From her "mount" she saw Tanner unzip the backpack and pull out a Polaroid camera and a small hand-held fan.

"All right, birthday girl," he said, circling around to the front of the pony, "get ready for the wind blowing back your flowing tresses as you gallop mightily through high mountain meadows." He held the small fan up in front of her face, and Kat flung her hair back so it could catch the "wind."

"Okay, smile!" Tanner said, holding up the camera with his other hand.

"Don't you dare!" Kat screamed, laughing and hiding her face.

"Oh, come on," Tanner pleaded, "be a sport."

"Fine," Kat muttered, pulling her hand away from her face, but she stuck out her tongue just as he took the picture.

"Nice," Tanner said, laughing. "That's a keeper." He put the developing picture on the floor next to the machine. The pony began slowing down, but before it stopped completely, Tanner slipped another coin into the slot and it began "galloping" again.

Tanner stepped back a few feet, folding his arms across his chest, watching her. "You look like a little girl on that."

Kat giggled. "I *feel* like a little girl!"

Tanner looked beyond her, out the window. "Speaking of little girls . . ." He nodded outside, and Kat turned to see a girl, five years old or so with long blond curls, staring longingly at the pony.

Kat looked back at Tanner. "Oh, we *have* to."

"Absolutely." Tanner cast a questioning glance at the child's mother, a woman in her early thirties with the same blond curls as her daughter except cut shorter. She nodded in delight. Tanner waved at the little girl to come inside, and her face broke out into an ecstatic smile.

As the little girl and her mother came in, Kat climbed down off the slowing ride.

The little girl rushed over to the pony, her blond curls bouncing around her shoulders. Hesitantly, she touched the pony's head, then looked up at Tanner hopefully.

Tanner smiled down at her. "Hi, I'm Tanner."

"I'm Ellie. May I have a ride please?"

Tanner put his finger on his chin contemplatively. "Hmm, I don't know, Ellie. That's a pretty big pony for such a little girl. Are you sure you can handle him?"

From a few feet away, Kat and Ellie's mother, who had introduced herself to Kat as Marcy, looked at each other, smiling.

"Yes!" Ellie burst out. "I *know* I can! Please, Mr. Tanner!"

"Well, all right then," Tanner said, feigning reluctance. "If you're sure." He bent down and swooped Ellie up into his arms, then set her down carefully on the pony.

She held on tight to the well-worn reins and kicked her feet against the sides of the still machine, her blue eyes shining in anticipation. Tanner plunked another coin into the slot, and the pony whirred and came back to life. Ellie squealed in delight, rocking back and forth twice as fast as the pony did. "Faster!" she screamed.

"Sorry," Tanner said with an apologetic shrug, "there's only one speed. Boy, little girls sure do like to go fast, don't they?" He gave Kat a wink, and she smiled at their shared joke.

"Do you and your husband have any children?" Marcy asked.

"Oh, he's not my husband," Kat said quickly, her eyes on Tanner, now holding up the mini-fan to blow back Ellie's curls. "We're just friends."

"Really," Marcy said with a knowing smile. "Are you sure about that? I saw the way he was looking at you."

Unexpectedly, the woman's comment sent a small thrill down the middle of Kat's spine. They both watched as Tanner took a picture of Ellie and put it down next to Kat's.

"He's pretty cute too," Marcy whispered, leaning closer to Kat. "Only don't tell my husband I said so—Oh, gosh." She gave a little jump and looked at her watch. "We've got to go." She took a step toward the ride. "Come on, cowgirl. Daddy's waiting."

"Sorry, kiddo," Tanner said, seeing the crushed look on Ellie's face. "Time to go." Despite her protests, he lifted her off the pony but then swung her around high in the air three times, and she screamed happily. All was forgiven.

Tanner put her down next to Marcy, then walked over to pick up the Polaroid of Ellie. "Here," he said, bending down on his knees to give it to her. "Now you'll always remember your special ride."

As Tanner ruffled her hair, Ellie suddenly leaned forward and wrapped her arms around his neck, kissing him solidly on the cheek. "Thank you *so* much!" she gushed before turning back to her mother. She took her hand and pulled her toward the door. "Did you see me, Mommy? Did you like my pony? I named him Happy. Do you think Mr. Tanner will marry me when I grow up?"

"Sorry, munchkin," Marcy said with a glance back at Kat. "I think he's already taken." As she let herself be pulled out the door, listening to her daughter's excited chatter, Marcy mouthed *Thank you* back at them.

After the door shut, Tanner and Kat smiled at each other, but Kat felt her lips tremble slightly. She realized she felt suddenly and inexplicably nervous being alone with him. Breaking eye contact, she looked around the empty store. "So, how'd you do this anyway? Get us in here?"

"I just called the leasing agent." Tanner nodded at the sign in the window. "After a little . . . finagling, she gave me the combination to the realtor's lockbox outside with the keys in it."

"Really," Kat said, impressed.

"Really." Tanner loaded the camera and fan back into the backpack, then walked over to the Polaroid snapshot of her. Leaning down to pick it up, he smiled up at her.

"I can be pretty persuasive when I want to be." Kat had absolutely no doubt about that. Tanner stood up and looked down at the picture, snorting out a laugh. "Now that *is* a keeper."

Kat groaned. "Let me see that." Walking over to him, she cringed when she caught sight of her expression. She had to admit, though, she'd never seen her eyes shine so brightly.

"Yep," Tanner said, heading for the door. "This here's some *serious* blackmail material."

"Give me that," Kat demanded, laughing as she reached to snatch it from him. But Tanner was too quick, raising the picture high over his head.

"Not so fast," he said, pushing the door open for her with his shoulder. Kat walked out backward, still trying to grab the picture.

"Oh, yeah," Tanner teased, "it's going to cost you big-time!"

"Uh-uh," Kat said, feeling like a little girl again as she reached up on tiptoe. But suddenly she lost her balance and with a small cry of surprise fell forward, her chest colliding heavily against his.

She regained her balance but didn't step away from him. Slowly Tanner lowered his arm, but Kat didn't try to grab the picture. Instead, she gazed up at him, saw his blue eyes steady on her.

"Thank you," she said softly. "This has been the best birthday I've ever had."

"You're very welcome." A small smile played at the corners of his lips. "Roomie."

And at that moment Kat realized she didn't care about the "roommates only" thing. Besides, it was her birthday, right? Maybe her present to herself would be to find out exactly how those lips felt against her own, and damn the consequences. It was just a kiss after all.

Her gaze fell to his mouth, and she saw his smile fade. A shiver of anticipation coursed down her spine as she closed her eyes and tilted her head up toward his.

But then Kat felt Tanner's entire body stiffen. She opened her eyes to see him gazing past her shoulder. "Looks like I've been a little outdone."

Frowning, Kat took a step back and followed his line of sight across the street. There stood Brian Winslow beside a horse-drawn carriage that could have rolled right out of the 1800s, complete with a pair of Clydesdales and a driver in a black top hat.

Brian held a bottle of Dom Perignon in one hand, a bouquet of red roses in the other. He had been smiling, but as Kat watched, his smile evaporated, his eyes moving back and forth between Kat and Tanner, his brows furrowing above his glasses. He'd probably just turned around a moment before. How much had he seen?

"Hi!" Kat said brightly, her face blazing as she walked across the street. Behind her, she heard Tanner locking up the SavMore. "What's all this?" she asked, taking in the ornate white and gold carriage.

But Brian didn't answer right away, his brown eyes now trained steadily on Tanner behind her.

"Brian? Did you hear me?" When he didn't answer her, Kat sighed, her smile faltering. She didn't like this situation one bit and felt helpless to make it better.

Finally Brian focused on her. "For your uh . . . birthday," he said, clearly uncomfortable. He took a deep breath and seemed to center himself. "I thought you deserved it. I know how hard you've been working." Kat winced at the bitter edge of irony in his tone. Across the street, she heard Tanner swear softly to himself, presumably having problems with the lockbox.

Brian cleared his throat and took her arm, turning his back to Tanner as if doing so would erase his existence. "And I know how much you love horses," he said with a tenuous smile, his light tone obviously forced.

It took a moment for Kat to realize that Brian was looking at her expectantly. "Oh," she said with a start. "Well, thank you so much!" She leaned forward to give him a light hug and a kiss on the cheek.

But Brian suddenly grasped her by the waist and pulled her toward him, angling his face toward hers. And then he was kissing her full on the mouth—hard, possessive, so unlike the light, quick kisses they'd always shared before.

Hearing Tanner approaching, Kat instinctively pulled away and took a step back from Brian, her lips throbbing. Tanner stopped a few feet away, unsmiling.

"Um, Brian," Kat began, her voice tight, "this is

Tanner McIntyre, the ranch foreman I told you about? And, Tanner, this is my editor, Brian Winslow."

Brian held out his right hand. "Nice to meet you— Tanner, was it?" Kat didn't like the snide tone that had crept into his voice.

Tanner didn't even make the attempt. "That's right," he said gruffly, shaking the other man's hand quick and hard. "Quite the getup you have here." He nodded toward the carriage and the horses, the one on the left shifting restlessly in his harness.

"Whoa, boy," the driver called softly as the carriage jerked forward.

"Well," Brian said, his tone patronizing, "it *is* Kat's thirtieth birthday after all."

"Really," Tanner said, moving toward the horses after an ironic glance back at Kat.

Kat sighed, wishing she could blow away the haze of testosterone hanging in the air.

Tanner approached the anxious horse and stroked the side of his head, murmuring into his ear. It worked. The carriage sat perfectly still as Brian helped Kat up into the plush velvet seat.

"I've made reservations at Quinn's," Brian said, sitting down next to her. "I had one heck of a time getting them. It'll be worth it, though. Best crème brulée in town." He leaned forward in the seat. "Driver," he called up to the man in the top hat.

But Kat touched his arm to stop him. "I'm sorry, Brian. I've already eaten."

"Oh," Brian said, clearly miffed. "Okay, how about a turn around the park then?"

"Great," Kat said, aware that Tanner, now stroking the other horse's neck, was listening to every word.

"Just around the park," Brian told the driver, who touched the brim of his hat. He lifted the reins, and the horses' heads rose in unison. Tanner stepped up onto the sidewalk as the driver made a clucking noise with his tongue.

"Oh, I'd better call and cancel the reservations," Brian muttered, taking out his cell phone. As he dialed the number, he glanced over at Tanner. "Nice meeting you, Tanner."

"You too," Tanner said in the same gruff voice as before.

As the carriage pulled away from the curb, Kat looked over at Tanner. Shadows crisscrossed his face, hiding his eyes, yet she knew he was looking right at her.

She felt it.

Chapter Twelve

"**I** think you know how I feel about you, Kat," Brian began when they'd reached a steady gait along Central Park West, the horses' hooves making crisp clip-clops against the asphalt of the street.

"Brian," Kat began, but she stopped when Brian put a hand on her knee and squeezed gently.

"Please, Kat, let me finish." He chuckled self-consciously. "I've been practicing." Kat sighed again and took a sip from her crystal Champagne flute. She didn't want to be having this conversation. "Look, I know we agreed to keep it light, but I just can't anymore. My feelings have gone way beyond any semblance of 'light.'"

And then Brian was pulling something from the inside pocket of his jacket, a small red box.

Cartier? Oh, no.

He knelt down in front of her on the floor of the carriage, and for some reason Kat noticed that his knee only hovered above the floor of the carriage, not actually touching it. The carriage jerked to one side as they hit a pothole, and Brian grabbed the seat behind him for balance. Once he was stable again, he smiled up at her, his eyes concealed behind the reflection of the streetlights in his glasses.

"I love you, Katherine Renee Callahan, and it would make me the happiest man in the world if you would do me the honor of becoming my wife." He opened the box and held it up to her. Inside was a stunning ring, three brilliant-cut diamonds, each one at least a carat, set in a gleaming platinum band. The ring took Kat's breath away. Literally.

"I know this comes as a bit of a surprise," Brian was saying as Kat tried to remember how to breathe, "and you don't have to say anything right now. Just know that it's out there. And, here, I'd like you to hold on to this for now."

He closed the box and slipped it into her hand as he sat back down next to her.

For a long moment Kat was quiet as she got used to the feel of the box in her hand. The clip-clops were seemingly louder now, echoing between the park wall and the exclusive stores across the street.

"Well," Brian finally said, clearing his throat nervously, "you don't seem exactly thrilled at the prospect." He took off his glasses and wiped the lenses with his handkerchief, which was monogrammed in dark blue stitching. Kat looked over at him and saw his eyes harden as he put them back on. "Is it the cowboy?"

"No," she said noncommitally, but she didn't have the energy to appease him further. Besides, it wouldn't have been honest. Tanner McIntyre was no longer just "the cowboy" to her. She didn't know exactly what he was, but he was *something*.

And the truth was, she *hadn't* been thinking about Tanner during her silence a moment earlier. She'd actually been envisioning how life would be with Brian.

Brian's job as an editor was merely a stepping stone to his future Upstairs. His family wanted him to get a feel for the business from the bottom up. He was on his way to big things.

Yes, life with Brian would certainly be fashionable, with the best of everything—his elegant brownstone, Broadway premieres, swanky cocktail parties, and, of course, dining out almost every night at Quinn's or Anon or wherever the "in" places were at the moment.

Kat thought then about the meal Tanner had cooked for her—the succulent steak, the grilled vegetables, the fluffy potatoes. She grinned, remembering Tanner's expression as he'd pulled one of the potatoes out of the embers and it had slipped through the tongs. He'd grabbed it before it could fall, then tossed it back and forth between his hands before finally getting it to Kat's plate, a true game of "hot potato."

"There's that smile I was looking for," Brian said

softly, turning Kat's face to kiss her lightly on the lips. He'd thought the smile had been for him.

All right, Kat thought with a sigh, turning to watch the passersby window-shop. So she did care about Tanner McIntyre. But he'd be going back to Colorado after his stay here, and Brian was here, a known factor. *Safe?* that little voice inside her whispered, although now it sounded suspiciously like Tanner's.

So what's wrong with safe? Kat countered the voice. Life with Brian would be so easy. And it would be nice to be taken care of. No one had really done that since her parents died.

And okay, so maybe she wasn't in love with Brian right now. But that could change, couldn't it? She could grow to love him. That used to happen all the time in arranged marriages. Those couples probably didn't have any butterflies either in the beginning, but they ended up happy in the long run. She could just skip to that part, the contentment. Maybe butterflies were overrated.

"Just think about it, okay?" Brian was asking. Kat turned to him, and now her smile *was* for him.

"I will, Brian," she said, relaxing back against his arm and taking another sip of Champagne. "I definitely will."

". . . then Winslow shows up with that ridiculous horse-and-buggy routine. Completely over the top." Luke laid back on the bed, his cell phone to his ear as he scowled up at the ceiling.

The voice on the other end of the line let out a soft chuckle. "Do I hear jealousy rearing its ugly head?"

"No!" Luke burst out, then sighed. "Yes. I guess. Damn, it wasn't supposed to happen this way. I'm completely out of control."

"Love has a way of doing that," the voice murmured, a hint of teasing coming through the words.

" 'Love'? Who said anything about love?"

Now came the soft chuckle again. "You did, honey."

"But I just met her!"

"Sometimes it's quick like that." Luke could almost see her shrugging those once-beautiful shoulders of hers, which had become so painfully thin over the last several months, the skin stretched taut against the bones. "So what *are* you going to do?"

"Nip it in the ol' bud," Luke answered, forcing a resolve into his voice he wasn't sure he felt.

"And how are you going to do that exactly?"

Luke's lips parted in an ironic smile. "Acting, my dear. It can't be *that* hard, can it?"

Again came that smooth chuckle. "Harder than you think."

From beside the bed, Lucy's ears pricked up as the front door of the condo opened. "I gotta go," he whispered, reaching over to turn off the bedside lamp. "She's back."

"All right. Oh, and, Luke?"

"Yeah?"

"Break a leg."

Now Luke sent his own wry chuckle through the phone line. "Thanks."

Kat closed the door, put her keys down, and headed for her room. In front of Tanner's door, though, she hesitated.

The door was closed, the slit underneath it dark. Her heart ached a little at the sight of it. She really just wanted to talk to him, work out her feelings, as if he were just a good friend and not *part* of it all.

She hadn't had a friend like that in a long time, hadn't felt comfortable enough with anyone—until Tanner came along. She felt she could say anything to him and it would be okay, accepted.

A soft thud came from inside his room, and Kat's heart sped up. She listened intently and sighed a moment later when she heard nothing further. Disappointment, unexpectedly deep, settled over her.

And in that moment she knew.

Kat put her hands on either side of the door and hung her head in reluctant acceptance. Despite all her defenses, despite all her resolve, it had happened, and she could no longer deny it.

Letting out a long, slow breath, Kat shook her head and turned to go into her room. She put the Cartier box in the top drawer of her vanity and sighed.

Why couldn't she just transfer her feelings for Tanner to Brian Winslow? That would solve everything.

* * *

Luke's eyes flew open at the sound of the board creaking as Kat hesitated just outside his door. His jaw tight, he turned to look at the doorknob, the brass glinting in the dim light from the window. He willed it to move, to turn and open and for Kat to come inside and walk over him.

Involuntarily his mind conjured up the image of that carriage and Brian Winslow standing next to it, his smug expression when he'd first turned around. Luke had gotten enormous satisfaction at Winslow's discombobulated look after seeing Luke and Kat together. But now he let out a deep breath.

He hadn't known it was so serious between Kat and Winslow. What Winslow had done tonight was proposal material—the carriage, the long-stemmed roses, expensive Champagne. . . . Luke chuckled sardonically, wondering if Winslow could take the silver spoon out of his mouth long enough to drink the fine wine.

His smile disappeared an instant later as the memory of Winslow grabbing Kat and kissing her so unexpectedly hard swept through his mind, vivid, real. His fists came crashing down on the mattress with an unsatisfyingly soft *whump!*

He'd barely been able to control himself at the sight of that kiss. It was all he could do not to rush over there and snatch Kat out of Winslow's puny, office-lazy arms.

His heart racing in fury, Luke took several deep breaths, and finally his hands relaxed at his sides as reason returned to him. He had no right to interfere in Kat's life. For him, Kat Callahan was a sweet fantasy, unattainable, like a doll in a glass case.

Still, though, Luke thought with a wry smile, turning his head again toward that agonizingly still doorknob, he wished that door would open. Then all bets would be off. But the floorboard creaked again, and a moment later he heard the soft click of her door closing.

Luke let out a long, frustrated breath and turned over onto his side. He'd created this situation, coming into Kat's life under false pretenses with the deliberate intention of manipulating her. But it had gone too far now. It wasn't right. It had never been right.

Yes, he had to undo some of the damage he'd done. And he knew exactly how to do it. Anger was easier to deal with than heartache, right? If it were going to work, though, it would have to be one heck of a performance. Academy Award-worthy.

Chapter Thirteen

Kat sighed as she opened the door of the condo the next evening. Working at Winslow hadn't been as easy today. All morning Brian had hovered around her office, an intense, questioning look constantly on his face as he waited for some sort of a reaction to his proposal.

Finally Kat had told him she wouldn't be able to really consider it until she was on vacation. That would be the best time anyway, away from both Brian and Tanner.

Brian had looked a little dejected at that, but at least he hadn't come by again until the end of the day to walk her to the elevator. His hurt-puppy expression didn't help his case at all.

Putting her things down, Kat pet both dogs and walked into the living room. She could hear the shower running in the guest room. Good, she thought, breathing out a sigh of relief as she headed down the hallway. She was nervous about seeing Tanner after the way he'd looked at her from the sidewalk when the carriage pulled away. She'd managed to avoid him that morning, sneaking out while he was walking the dogs.

As Kat walked into the kitchen, she heard the shower turn off. He'd be out any minute now. Kat had no idea how he would act toward her. Would he be angry? Sad? Indifferent? And she had no clue how she'd be with him.

After a moment spent perusing the menus on the refrigerator, Kat decided for once that she was in the mood to cook. She wanted the distraction. Nothing fancy, though.

She took out the half package of angel hair pasta, the leftover marinara sauce, and an Italian sausage. After setting a pot to boil, she began slicing up the sausage. The knife slipped on the cutting board when she heard Tanner's door open.

"Hi there," he said, striding into the kitchen, his voice surprisingly cheerful. Kat hadn't expected that.

"Hi," she said, trying to match his tone. "I'm making some 'skinny spaghetti.' Interested?"

"No, thanks." Tanner opened the refrigerator and grabbed the carton of orange juice.

"You don't know what you're missing," Kat warned, throwing the sausage slices into a frying pan.

Tanner came up next to her, and Kat got out of the way as he opened the cupboard above her and reached for a glass. Unable to help herself, Kat moved back a little closer to him and breathed in his freshly showered smell, the clean, masculine scent of his shampoo. A drop of water dribbled off the end of one wet curl and landed on her shoulder. Kat shivered at the unexpected dot of coolness there.

"Sorry," Tanner said gruffly, wiping her shoulder with his thumb. His touch sent tingles racing down her spine.

Tanner poured himself a glass of juice, put the carton back, and walked to the kitchen table.

"Look, Kat, I've been thinking," he began, pulling out a chair and sitting down. "You were right."

Kat turned to him, again surprised at his tone but now because of how serious it was. His expression was also somber as he took a sip of juice.

"About what?" Kat asked lightly, smiling. She decided she didn't like this new, unknown side of Tanner. Her smile fading, she turned back to her sausage.

"About what you said about our being strictly roommates," Tanner answered. "I realized that last night. And I'll admit I was looking for a way around it."

"Really," Kat said automatically, a prickly feeling forming in her stomach, as if the butterflies in there were developing tiny spikes on their wings.

"Uh-huh," Tanner said. Kat heard him sip his orange juice before letting out a breath. She sensed he had more to say, but she suddenly didn't want to hear any more.

"You're just so incredibly attractive, I couldn't help myself." He chuckled, but Kat thought it sounded forced. "And sexy as hell. But, well, I'm not really into relationships, you know? And you deserve more than that—more than somebody like me, who's really only after one thing."

Kat's stomach lurched, and she had to look away from the sausage in the pan. It suddenly nauseated her. She forced herself to breathe calmly, evenly. In and out. In and out.

Still, though, tears sprang into her eyes, and she blinked quickly, but one escaped. She swiped it away, trying hard not to sniffle.

"Anyway," Tanner was saying, "I realized last night that maybe that wasn't clear between us, and I didn't want you to get hurt. I figured we were on the same page, though, given our situation, but I just wanted to be sure. *And* I didn't realize how serious things were between you and Winslow—Brian. Now *he* seems like a good guy, someone who *does* deserve you."

He was quiet for a moment, and Kat again felt he had more to say. This time she was glad about that, glad she didn't need to say anything at that moment, her throat so constricted, it felt caught in a vise.

"I just hope I didn't mess things up for you last night," Tanner was saying. "Brian didn't seem very happy about . . . well, seeing whatever it was he saw."

Aware she needed to say something now, Kat swallowed hard and took in a deep breath. "Oh, no," she said with a wave of the spatula, feigning nonchalance pretty darn well, she thought. "He was fine about it. And don't worry about me and you. We were—*are*—definitely on the same page."

"Well, good, then." Tanner chuckled, and this time it seemed more natural. "And I promise you, no more cheap ploys like that whole ranch-on-the-roof bit."

It was like a stab at Kat's heart. The single best night of her life had been a "cheap ploy"? Tears stung her eyes, and a sniffle snuck in, but Kat thought the crackling of the grease in the pan drowned it out. She blinked her eyes fiercely to squelch the tears.

Tanner's chair squeaked against the floor as he got up. Thank God he was going. She didn't know much longer she could maintain this act.

"So anyway, I just wanted to let you know that I'll leave you alone from now on. For real."

Kat only nodded, pretending to concentrate on her sausage. Out of the corner of her eye she saw him looking at her as he leaned against the sink. He seemed to be expecting her to say something. But, really, what else *was* there to say after his little speech?

Gripping the spatula hard, she turned to him, forcing a casual smile. "Are you sure you don't want any of this?" she asked, even raising her eyebrows questioningly.

Tanner shook his head. "Nope. But thanks." He drained his glass and rinsed it out. As he leaned down to put it into the dishwasher, he gave her a sidelong smile. "Actually, I was thinking about paying a visit to my favorite new neighbor."

He closed the dishwasher and came closer to Kat,

nudging her playfully in the elbow. "And I don't mean old Mrs. Burgstrom." And then, to Kat's utter astonishment, Tanner actually winked at her, his lips curling into a lascivious grin.

Kat could only stare blankly at him, speechless, not caring that the grease from the sausage was starting to burn, spattering up in loud bursts, the spray of it stinging her hand and wrist like a hundred tiny needles.

"You'd better watch that," Tanner said, nodding down at the pan. Without another word he sidled out of the kitchen, then whistled his way down the hallway. A moment later Kat heard the front door open and close.

In a daze, she turned off the flame from under both the sausage and boiling water, her appetite now nonexistent. She walked to the kitchen table and sat down in a heap, her face in her hands as she tried to wrap her mind around what Tanner had just said to her.

She especially couldn't believe the way he'd talked to her at the end, as if she were one of the swarthy men from the bunkhouse on his ranch, as if he'd never cared about her at all.

But he hadn't, had he? He'd just told her that himself. He'd never cared about *her,* Kat Callahan. He'd only been after "one thing."

Kat thought back over the last several days. Everything—their intimate talks, the rooftop ranch, the pony ride—were all part of Tanner's plan to get her into bed?

Anger, fierce and sharp, flared up in Kat, and her

hands gathered into tight fists on the table. She'd actually thought she'd begun falling in *love* with the man. She didn't even *know* him! This new Tanner was utterly foreign to her. If she *had* fallen in love, it would have been with a sham.

Damn him! Kat's fists banged hard against the table, jarring the salt and pepper shakers. Why did he have to come into her life? She hadn't known she could feel so strongly about someone, and now . . .

Letting out a breath, Kat stood up and automatically began cleaning up her uneaten dinner, pouring out the boiling water and scraping the sausage into the disposal.

It made a satisfying grating noise as it went down the drain.

Kat's heart thundered in her chest as she walked quickly toward her building, a block away now. Was he still back there? She was afraid to look.

The man in the blue Windbreaker was following her again, although now he wore a faded gray T-shirt. Still, Kat had been fairly certain it was the same man, leaning against the bank across the street from Winslow's main entrance, sipping a cup of coffee and reading the newspaper—or pretending to anyway.

Hoping she'd made a mistake, Kat had kept an eye on the man as she'd headed toward the subway stairs. He hadn't moved an inch. But then she'd spotted him in the subway car behind hers. He must have sprinted to the stairs and climbed aboard the car at the last minute.

Luckily, it had been rush hour, the subway cars packed with people. Still, when she'd gotten off at her station, she was glad to see a transit cop talking to the pretty blonde who worked in the token booth. But just as Kat had approached him, the cop had sprinted off after a fare jumper.

Now a half block from her house, Kat slowed a little. She had to know if the man was still following her. She hadn't seen him in the station, but he could have been hiding behind any of the thick pillars down there. Holding her breath, Kat glanced backward, scanning the street behind her.

And there he was, standing on the other side of the intersection, partially hidden in a small crowd of pedestrians and still feigning interest in the paper as he waited for the light to change.

The light did change then, and the man tucked the paper under his arm and continued forward. Toward Kat.

She spun around. Had he seen her looking at him? Who was he? Just a creepy but harmless admirer? Or something more sinister? What if he were just waiting for an opportunity to—to . . . God only knew what.

Beginning to panic now, Kat half ran toward her building, her eyes searching desperately for a cop or anyone who could help her. Normally her street bustled with activity at this time of the evening, but at the moment it seemed almost deserted, only an elderly man with a cane two buildings up and a young mother pushing a stroller across the street. Kat was on her own.

Would this be the opportunity the man had been waiting for all along?

Finally reaching the steps of her building, Kat plunged her hand into her purse, her fingers grasping for her keys. Oh, why didn't she put them in the same compartment every time instead of throwing them in any which way?

Distracted, Kat almost tripped going up the steps, but finally her fingers seized on the keys. With a rush of relief she yanked them out, fumbled for the key to the front door, then jammed it into the lock. Of course it didn't turn right away. She worked it back and forth, but it stubbornly refused to budge.

"Damn it!" Kat cried out in sheer desperation. Was he coming up the steps behind her even now, gun poised to shove into her ribs, drag her inside . . .

But just then the front door opened, and there was Tanner with the dogs, followed by Jackie.

"Oh, Tanner, thank God!" Kat burst out breathlessly, clutching his arm. "That man. I saw him by the Winslow building and in the subway. And now here."

"Where?" Tanner demanded. Kat turned, scanning the street, but she didn't spot him right away.

"That way," Kat said, pointing to the last place she'd seen him. "Pretending to read the paper."

"I see him," Tanner said with a curt nod. He thrust the dogs' leashes into Kat's hand, then ran down the steps and across the street.

"What's going on?" Jackie asked, her eyes wide with fear, as Kat's probably were.

"A man's been following me," Kat explained distractedly, still looking for the man. And then she saw him, leaning against the furniture store across the street, three buildings up.

At that moment he looked up from his paper, his eyes widening as he saw Tanner closing in on him fast. The man threw down the paper and took off, heading for the alley several yards away. With a burst of speed, Tanner followed him, disappearing into the alley behind him.

"Oh, no," Kat muttered to herself, her breaths quick and shallow. What if the man really did have some kind of weapon—a knife or a gun? Tanner would be totally defenseless! She couldn't just stand there. She had to *do* something.

"Take them," she commanded Jackie, almost throwing her the leashes. She crossed the street haphazardly, a taxi honking angrily at her, and ran toward the alley, not knowing what she'd do once she got there.

Or what she'd find.

"I'm sorry," the man said, shaking his head and breathing hard from their short sprint. "She must've spotted me."

Luke grunted. "You think? Never mind. Seriously, though, you're through. Here."

Reaching into his back pocket, he drew out his wallet, counted out ten bills, and shoved them into the man's hand. "Thanks for all your help." Luke's sarcasm was lost on the man, his eyes widening at the small stack of cash.

"No problem. Give me a call if you need anything else."

"I'll get right on that."

This time Luke's tone came through loud and clear. The man scowled, opening his mouth to utter some undoubtedly witty and insightful rejoinder, but then he shrugged, tucking the money into his jacket pocket. "Whatever," he mumbled before half jogging down the rest of the alley.

Luke let out a breath, turning around to head back toward the entrance to the alley. "Good riddance."

Kat stopped next to the entrance to the alley, took a deep breath, then rounded the corner. And ran right into Tanner. She burst out into a shrill scream, her nerves raw.

"Tanner, you scared me! Are you all right?"

"I'm fine," he mumbled, leaning over and putting his hands on his knees to catch his breath. "That man must be half antelope. He got away."

"I'm just glad you're okay," Kat said.

Both still breathing hard, they headed back toward Jackie and the dogs. "What do you think he wants from me?" Kat wondered aloud as they crossed the street. She drew in a sharp breath and grabbed Tanner's arm. "Do you think it could have something to do with my book? I mean—"

"Damn that book!" Tanner suddenly exploded, jerking his arm away.

Kat took a step back from him, completely dumbfounded by the vehemence in his voice, the fury in his eyes.

"Why do you care so much about it anyway?" he demanded. "It's a waste of time! It's *trash*! Don't you get that? And the only people who'll read it are *trash*!"

Now Kat felt her anger rising to meet his. "What, and I'm *trash* for writing it?" She planted her hands on her hips, her head cocked to one side.

"You said it, not me," Tanner grumbled, turning away from her.

Kat stared after him as he marched away, shaking her head in disbelief as she tried to grasp what had just happened. First the man following her, then Tanner's inexplicable tirade.

When he reached Jackie, Tanner grabbed the leashes.

"Are you all right?" Kat heard Jackie ask, her voice anxious.

Tanner gave her a curt nod. "Yeah. Let's go." As Tanner began walking briskly toward the park, Jackie hesitated, glancing back at Kat, confusion clear in her heavily lined eyes. Then she shrugged and ran a few steps to catch up with Tanner.

As she watched Jackie take his arm, a pang of jealousy struck Kat hard, but she forced herself to remember her conversation with Tanner, what she'd begun to think of as their "one thing" talk. And surely Jackie wasn't looking for a long-term anything either. Really, they were made for each other, weren't they?

Her cell phone rang then, and she pulled it out of her purse. "Hello?" she answered, her jaw still tight.

"Wow, what did *I* do?"

"Oh, sorry, Brian," Kat said, forcing her jaw to ease. "It's not you."

"Good to hear."

Kat glanced down the street and saw Tanner put his arm around Jackie's waist. Her shoulders stiffening, she turned away from them. Instilling a light tone into her voice she asked, "Hey, you free for dinner?"

"Are you kidding? Definitely!"

Kat cringed at his little-boy eagerness but tried to get past it.

"Great. Pick me up in a half hour."

Without another glance down the street, Kat walked up the stairs of her building to get ready for dinner.

Chapter Fourteen

"**P**hew," Kat exhaled, collapsing against the black leather seat of the limo. "I'm glad *that's* over. Thank God for your grandfather's dirty martinis!"

Brian chuckled as he slid in beside her and the driver closed the door. "You did just fine, honey. They loved you."

"I'm sure it helped that I finished the revisions early," Kat said pointedly.

"I'm glad you did. With the DNA results coming in tomorrow, they really would've been on you. I've never seen them *this* excited about a new release. They're like little kids on Christmas morning! All thanks to you."

He patted her knee, covered in sumptuous off-black stockings.

Kat had gone all out for this night, spending an exorbitant amount of money on the stockings, a new cocktail dress, and gorgeous Manolo Blahnik's.

She'd also sat for two hours at a salon having her hair styled in a tight French twist and getting her makeup done, even splurging on a manicure *and* pedicure. She'd wanted to feel the part, feel as if she belonged at the Winslow mansion, one of the oldest and largest residences on the Upper East Side.

Brian had wanted to introduce Kat to his family and so had arranged the dinner party. It was an intimidating prospect, knowing she'd be surrounded by fifteen impeccably dressed Winslows, all eager to meet her, especially the patriarch of the family, Winslow Publishing's CEO, Basil Winslow.

Yet despite her extravagant spending, Kat couldn't shake the feeling she was still only playing a part, getting into costume for a play or a Halloween party. After two of Basil's dirty martinis, though, she'd felt she could at least hold her own with the powerful family when they'd finally sat down to dinner in the elegant main hall of the mansion.

She needn't have been so nervous, though. There were no awkward lulls in the conversation. Now that she'd finished the revisions, the Janssen book was the hot topic. The Winslows expected it to debut at number one. And Brian's father, seated next to her, seemed genuinely interested in what Kat had to say about possible marketing strategies, even though a massive national campaign was already in the works.

It certainly didn't hurt that the Janssens had been garnering even more publicity themselves over the last week and a half. The media firestorm over their disappearance had only increased with each passing day.

Due to intense pressure from the media, the LA police chief had held a press conference, assuring the public that the Janssens had been in touch with him and that they were fine and were simply choosing not to let their whereabouts be known. He emphasized that they had every right to do that.

His assurances had done little to quell the frenzy, though, and so, wanting to take advantage of the mountain of free publicity, Winslow Publishing had put the book on the fast track for publication—assuming, of course, that the DNA results came in on time.

The Winslows had been ecstatic to hear that Kat had finished ahead of schedule. The last week and a half she'd thrown herself into the work, eager to get it done so she could fly away to Colorado and be done with Tanner once and for all. She'd found avoidance the best way to cope with him—a fairly easy task, as Tanner seemed to want the same thing.

They'd developed a routine in which they rarely crossed each other's path. As Tanner slept in, Kat would walk the dogs, then leave for Winslow, and Tanner would walk them at night so Kat could work late. Not wanting to come home, she'd taken Brian up several times on his offers of late dinners out.

His appeal had grown exponentially since Tanner's

"one thing" revelation, and Kat had allowed herself to more fully explore the possibility of life as a Winslow. And if today's pampering at the salon were any indication of how that would be, she could definitely get used to it.

"You look so beautiful tonight," Brian murmured into her ear as he lay an arm across her shoulders, "I don't want to let you go just yet. Why don't you come over for a nightcap? Or some coffee?" He caressed Kat's bare upper arm lightly with his fingertips. "Please?" Was that a tingle she felt there? She thought it just might have been.

Seeing Brian tonight in his element, so relaxed and confident among such powerful people and amid such enormous wealth, had shown her a new side of him, one she found very attractive, even sexy.

"Besides," Brian was saying, "I'm not going to get to see you for two whole weeks while you're out West doing your little cowgirl thing."

Kat bristled at his condescension, her shoulders stiffening under his arm. She was seeing that—his condescension—much too often. They would definitely have to have a talk about that. Not tonight, though, Kat decided. She was happy with how things had gone at dinner and didn't want to ruin her good mood.

"All right," Kat said as the limo pulled up in front of her building. "I'd love some coffee. Decaf, though. My nerves are already pretty wired from tonight. Let me just run upstairs and check on Oliver."

"Why don't you bring him with you?" Brian suggested. "It's high time we introduced him to Goldie." Brian's dog, Goldie, was a retired show dog, an elegant afghan with a luxurious tan coat that always had a just-groomed sheen to it.

Kat laughed. "Talk about the prince and the pauper."

Brian gave her a quick, hesitant smile. "Oliver *is* neutered, isn't he?"

"Of course!" Kat answered, indignant and hoping her voice conveyed that.

"Well, come on, sweetheart," Brian said with a placating smile, "we wouldn't want *little* princes and paupers running around now, would we?"

"I guess not," Kat murmured, her jaw a little tight. She started to get out of the limo, but Brian stopped her with a light touch on her knee. Kat turned back and saw a new gleam in his brown eyes.

"Just don't change out of that dress. I'm not done looking at you in it yet." His eyes took in the simple black silk dress Kat had bought the day before at the Ralph Lauren boutique on Madison Avenue. She'd thought it a bit short, but the saleswoman had assured Kat that it was the perfect length for a cocktail dress. And it had been. The dress Brian's younger sister, Sarah, had worn tonight had been even shorter, and no one seemed to think twice about it.

"Oh," Brian said as Kat climbed out onto the sidewalk. "And give the cowboy a big howdy-do for me, will you?"

Kat gave Brian a perfunctory smile, then walked toward the stairs as the driver closed the limo's door. Since he'd met Tanner on the night of Kat's birthday, Brian had made at least one snide comment about him every day. Kat didn't like it but decided it wasn't worth talking to him about. Soon Tanner would no longer be a part of her life, and it would be a moot point.

Still, though, Kat thought as she impatiently jiggled her key in the front door of her building, jealousy was a side of Brian she found neither attractive nor sexy.

Tanner was in the kitchen. Kat could hear him rustling around in there.

"I'm home," she called to him as she greeted the dogs. She heard Tanner mumble something in acknowledgment but couldn't make out the words.

Reaching into the bowl, Kat grabbed Oliver's leash and pulled it out, only to find it all tangled up with Lucy's. *Shoot.*

"I finished the revisions today," she called again as she untangled the leashes. "I couldn't get a flight out tomorrow, so I'll be leaving the day after. You'll finally have the place to yourself."

"Great," was his response. Then came the sound of a newspaper page turning.

Kat yanked out the last knot and clipped the freed leash onto Oliver's collar. "Sorry, Luce, you're sitting this one out." Lucy seemed to understand, her tail drooping a few inches. "Better get used to it," Kat muttered matter-of-factly as she pet the adoring dog. "Oh, and I'd better bring some treats for you," she said to Oliver. She might need something to bribe him with if he started acting up around Goldie.

Unfortunately, that meant going into the kitchen.

Kat took a deep breath and headed down the hall, both dogs trailing along behind her, Oliver's leash dragging on the floor.

Tanner was eating a bowl of cereal at the kitchen table, the newspaper spread out in front of him. Averting her eyes, Kat headed directly for the cupboard where she kept Oliver's food. In her peripheral vision she saw Tanner glance up at her.

Instantly his spoon clattered into the bowl, the milk splashing up in all directions. Kat stopped and turned to face him. She hadn't seen him in two days and was surprised by how rough he looked, his hair a mass of unruly dark curls, his face obviously unshaven since she'd seen him last. She couldn't help but notice how the thick stubble emphasized the sharp angles of his cheekbones.

He wore a wrinkled chambray shirt that matched his eyes perfectly, the blue of them jumping out vividly from between those two dark lines of lashes.

"What?" she asked at his open stare. Tanner blinked, then looked back down at the table.

"Nothing," he muttered, his voice gruff. "I've just never seen you dressed up before." And then, barely audibly, he added, "You look nice." Picking up his napkin, he began mopping up the spatters of milk from around the bowl.

"Oh," Kat said, suddenly feeling self-conscious. She'd forgotten what she was wearing. "Well, thanks."

Tanner shrugged indifferently, then stood, picked up his bowl and spoon, and carried them to the sink.

"I'm going over to Brian's for some coffee," she told him as she headed toward the dog food cupboard. "And I'm taking Oliver. Brian wants him to meet his dog, Goldie." Kat had no idea why she'd added the last part.

She opened the cupboard and took out the bag of Milk-Bones, then stood, meaning to go to the drawer on the other side of the sink, where she kept the Ziploc bags. She didn't realize Tanner had opened the dishwasher door, though, and she walked right into it, her right shin smacking hard against the sharp edge.

"Ow!" she cried out, grasping the counter for support as her heels twisted underneath her. She kicked off the expensive shoes angrily, swearing under her breath as she closed her eyes against the intensity of the pain.

"You're bleeding," Tanner said, and Kat opened her eyes to look down at her leg. A line of bright red was absorbing into the dark silk.

"Dang it," she muttered, seeing a tear in the stocking. "They're ruined."

Tanner closed the dishwasher door. "I'll get you a Band-Aid. Where do you keep them?"

"In my bathroom," Kat told him, "in the cabinet behind the mirror."

As Tanner walked out of the room, Kat limped to the kitchen table. "Shoot, shoot, shoot," she grumbled, aware that Brian was waiting for her downstairs.

While Tanner was out of the room, she quickly unsnapped both the stockings and rolled them off. She'd just have to put her shoes on her bare feet.

Looking up as Tanner came back into the kitchen, Kat was surprised to see him smiling. She hadn't seen that in at least a week and had forgotten how perfect and white his teeth were.

"Barney?" he asked, holding up the purple box of bandages.

Oh, no. "They were on sale," she said, and she cringed at the defensiveness in her voice. "When SavMore closed. A quarter a box."

"Not bad," Tanner said with an impressed nod as he knelt down in front of her. He'd also brought in a bottle of peroxide and a cotton ball, which he wet, then dabbed gingerly against the cut. The bleeding had slowed, but the pain still came in short, sharp throbs.

Kat grimaced, suddenly feeling five years old—a sensation reaffirmed a moment later as Tanner took out one of the Barney bandages, peeled off the backing, and pressed the flaps onto either side of the cut.

"There you go," he said with a satisfied nod. "Good as new." But then he sat back on his heels and examined his work more critically. "Although not quite as color coordinated, I have to say."

Kat raised her leg to look down at the purple bandage.

It did look odd with the elegant black dress. "Ralph Lauren would sic the fashion police on me if he saw this." Looking back at Tanner, she saw the laughter building up behind his smile, and suddenly she couldn't suppress a giggle herself. It was nice sharing a laugh with him. Too nice.

As their laughter died away, Kat saw something change in Tanner's blue eyes. Darn it, he wasn't *allowed* to look at her that way anymore, that way of his that seemed to see right through her outer shell, past every last one of her defenses.

"Well, I should get going." She stood up and limped toward the bag of Milk-Bones still on the floor next to the dishwasher. She leaned down and grabbed it but didn't realize Tanner had come up behind her. She jumped when she felt his left hand lightly clasp her waist. She froze. "Please, don't," she heard herself say through an eruption of tingles beneath his fingertips.

But Tanner ignored her plea as he reached over with his other hand and slowly, deliberately took the bag from her, setting it back down on the floor.

Waging an internal battle between *shoulds* and *shouldn'ts,* Kat drew in a long breath and laid her hands on the countertop in front of her, hoping to pull some strength from the cold hardness of the tile. Right now she had none.

And then, behind her, she felt Tanner carefully pull out the comb holding her French twist, and her hair came tumbling down around her shoulders. He reached up with both hands and gathered up her curls in his fingers tenderly, lovingly, as if they were strands of real gold.

"I'm sorry," Tanner whispered, "I just can't . . . *not.*" And then she felt his breath warm and high on her neck just before he drew her earlobe in between his lips, gently nibbling around the small pearl of her earring. Kat let out a rush of air.

Tanner pulled back from her and slowly turned her around to face him. For a moment he only gazed at her, exploring her face as if seeing it for the first time. And then Kat saw desire film over the blue of his eyes as his gaze fell to her mouth. He seemed to explore there also, as if memorizing every curve, every line. Slowly he brushed the tip of his tongue along first his lower lip, then the upper, wetting them.

Kat's heart fluttered in anticipation as Tanner leaned forward, his lips parting. And this time she didn't even think of stopping him. She closed her eyes, took in a breath, and a moment later felt the warm, soft touch of his lips against hers, gentle and intimate, slow and patient.

"Oh, Kat, Kat," he murmured before desire took over, his gentleness giving way to it, his lips working harder against hers, the feel of the kiss becoming more urgent for both of them.

God help her, she didn't even care about . . .

"Brian," she said, her voice barely above a whisper. Instantly Tanner stiffened, and he jerked away from her.

Kat opened her eyes to see him glaring down at her, his blue eyes blazing.

"Winslow? Damn him!"

Oh, Lord, he'd misunderstood. "No, I—"

"Does he touch you like I do?" Tanner interrupted. "Does he kiss you like—" Cutting off his own words, Tanner yanked her to him, his lips now crushing hers, claiming her mouth as his. His hands flew to her hair, kneading the strands harder than before.

But as difficult as it was to do, Kat laid her hands on his chest, pressing, urging him back. After a moment he finally did pull away, and he looked down at her expectantly, demanding. "I have to call Brian," she managed, her voice raspy and gruff, sounding alien to her. "He's waiting for me."

Tanner's eyes darkened at the sound of the name, but he nodded almost imperceptibly and walked to the cordless phone, lying in its cradle on the far side of the counter. He picked it up and walked back to her, holding the phone out expectantly.

Her hand trembling, Kat took the phone from him and just held it for a moment, taking in several deep breaths, trying to regain some sense of composure before she made the call.

For the moment, Tanner left her alone, walking over to the dogs lying by the kitchen table. He pet them both and whispered softly to them as he waited.

Kat drew in one more deep breath, pushed the speed dial button, and waited for the connection to go through.

"Hi, Brian, it's me." Her voice sounded forced, strained. She swallowed hard, her eyes on Tanner as he stood up and headed back over to her. A small teasing smile now played at the corners of his lips.

"Hi, hon', what's up?" Brian asked. "Where are you?" Concern tinged his voice, but Kat thought she also heard a hint of suspicion, as if he could sense what was happening three stories above him.

"I'm sorry," Kat said, now sounding remarkably normal despite the fact that Tanner was staring openly at her mouth as he made a show of licking his lower lip, swollen from their crushing kiss, as hers probably was.

She needed to concentrate. Turning around, she placed one hand on the cold realness of the countertop.

"But when I got here," she continued, trying to breathe evenly, "I got hit with a wave of exhaustion, probably from all the stress I was feeling about dinner tonight. I think I'm just going to call it a night and get some sleep."

"Oh," Brian said after a long hesitation, disappointment clear in his voice. "All right. Well, I guess I'll just see you tomorrow, then."

"Absolutely," Kat said, a bit too enthusiastically, happy to be almost through with this uncomfortable conversation. But Tanner showed her no mercy. She heard him come up behind her, felt the heat radiating from him even before he placed his hands on her waist and slowly spun her around.

Her heart thudding, Kat looked down at his chest, trying desperately to focus on the phone call. Still, she felt her own body heat responding to Tanner's, could almost see it churning between them.

Reaching up, Tanner turned her chin so she was forced to look at him. "Say good-bye," he mouthed, a wicked glint in his eyes.

"You were phenomenal tonight," Brian was saying, his voice softer now. "They all loved you." He chuckled lightly. "I have to say, I was a little nervous too. I mean, I know you're not used to . . . well, they're not exactly your kind of people, are they?"

"Say good-bye," Tanner repeated, above a whisper now. Panicked but oddly thrilled at the same time, Kat held her hand over the mouthpiece and glared at him. Tanner ignored it, mischief gleaming in his eyes as he held out his hand for the phone.

"Say . . ." he began in a tone dangerously close to normal volume.

"Okay," Kat said quickly, "See you tomorrow, then. Good night." As she jabbed down the End button, she could barely hear Brian's tinny-sounding, "Good night," but could still make out in it a stronger edge of suspicion. She wasn't sure she cared anymore, though, especially after his "they're not your kind of people" comment.

Still, she took a pretend swat at Tanner as he took the phone from her. "You had no right to do that," she said, but she knew her grin defused any force behind the words.

"I know," Tanner said, walking to the phone's console and hanging it up. He gave her a mock sheepish shrug as he came back to her. "But I'm like that."

"I like the way you are," she whispered. He looked at her mouth for a long moment in that studious way of his, then tilted his head forward and brushed his lips across hers once, then again, before leaning in to kiss her full on the mouth, though not with the crushing passion of before but tenderly now and unexpectedly sweet. Kat let herself fall into the kiss with her entire being, abandoning herself to it, savoring the feel of it, of him.

"Oh, Tanner," she murmured into his mouth.

Abruptly he pulled back from her, taking in a harsh breath.

"Damn it all," he grumbled, turning away from her and raking both hands through his dark curls.

"What's wrong?" Kat asked, reaching for him, but he took another step away from her. "Tanner?" He flinched then, almost as if she'd slapped him. What the . . . ?

"I'm sorry, this was a mistake," he said, his voice so gruff, so guttural, it barely sounded like words, more animal-like, pure emotion.

And then he was gone. She heard his footsteps move down the hall to the living room, heard the springs of the couch as he sat down. The dogs rose and followed him. She watched them, her lips still throbbing from his kiss, her heart aching. What was going on? She had to know. Taking a deep breath, she walked out into the living room.

Tanner hadn't bothered turning on the lamp. Still, Kat could see him in the light coming through the blinds from the street lamps outside, horizontal lines splashed on the far wall. Neon light from the Danforth Hotel on the corner striped the ceiling in steady, even pulses of red.

Tanner's back was to her, his head in his hands, his shoulders tensed. She came up behind him, then spoke hesitantly. "Tanner?"

His shoulders jerked, again as if she'd struck him. He let out a long breath and lowered his hands. Slowly he raised his head but didn't look at her, instead staring straight ahead.

Kat walked around the couch and followed his line of sight to her picture on the mantel, the one with Charlie the Clydesdale. A band of light crossed the center of the picture, lighting up her pouting face.

Kat turned back to him and saw that Tanner was looking at her now, a small, complicated smile just barely curling up the corners of his mouth. He reached for her hand and gently pulled until she was sitting next to him. He looked at her face for a long moment, then lay his fingertips against her temple and skimmed down the contours of her face—her cheekbone, the line of her jaw, her chin. His touch was so light, it felt like a warm breath. "God help me, I don't care anymore." His hands fell to her waist, and he pulled her toward him. "Come 'ere, you."

And then he was kissing her, with neither the hard

brutality nor the tender lightness of before. Now it was in between, his lips kneading hers, gentle but insistent, passionate but not in the least bit demanding.

She fell into the kiss, relishing the feel of those soft, firm lips against hers, realizing she'd been waiting for this every second of every minute of every day since that horrible day in the kitchen.

Chapter Fifteen

"You were right, you know," she murmured against his neck a while later and immediately felt his chuckle against her cheek.

"I usually am."

"Ha-ha."

"So what was I right about this time?"

Kat let out a breath, her grin fading. "The thing you said that made me so mad. About the book. It *is* trash. My mother would be horrified that it's my first published book."

"Really."

Kat nodded. "She was a ninth grade English teacher. P.S. 109 in the Bronx." She tilted her head to look up at the ceiling, watching the splashing red light from the

Danforth. She always thought there was something soothing about it, the steadiness of it.

"She loved teaching—helping her kids 'find their voices,' she called it. And when she saw how much I loved writing, she encouraged me too. She read everything I wrote, always urging me to write from my heart, even when I was little and just making up silly stories."

Kat smiled sadly as she remembered. "She said that early on she recognized in me the same thing she saw in my dad—an ability to see another level in the world, a richer, more complex level, and then be able to express it, only I used words instead of paint. It was the quality that had drawn her to my dad in the first place. She loved that I had it too and thought Andrea might but 'just hadn't found her medium yet,' as she put it."

And then it was too late, Kat thought but didn't say out loud. As it was she could feel the ever-close tears brewing behind her eyes. She swallowed hard before continuing. "Anyway, about the Janssen book, it was supposed to be a means to an end—and I'm not talking about money." Kat glanced over at Tanner, who was looking at her, intently listening.

She let out a mirthless chuckle. "Kind of like a criminal pulling one last job so he can start the legit business he'd always dreamed of."

"Is that how you see it?" Tanner asked with a quizzical look. "Like a crime?"

Kat shrugged, thinking about it. "I don't know—morally maybe. I mean, I really do believe what I said about celebrities using the media as much as the media uses them. . . ." She shrugged again, a little guiltily this time. "But Victoria Janssen *did* get out of the business to concentrate on being a mom. And yes, maybe she *does* have something to hide, a mistake, but does she deserve to have a whole book written about it? And that little boy . . ."

Kat was quiet for a long moment, her stomach tightening as the thoughts she'd kept at bay for so long came back to haunt her.

"So tell me," Tanner said, his voice soft. "What *was* the 'end' you were talking about? If not money?"

Kat sighed and looked back up at the ceiling. "Well, ever since college, I've been working on a novel—one that *would* have made my mother proud. I worked on it in my spare time when I wasn't doing freelance articles. It was"—Kat laughed self-consciously—"precious to me, almost like a baby—except with a decade-long labor."

"Ouch."

Kat nodded, smiling. "But worth it, I think. I finished it just a few weeks ago. And I was about to print it out for the first time."

"The first time?" Tanner repeated, raising his eyebrows.

Kat let out a self-deprecating chuckle as she nodded. "I don't know, it was just so fragile to me, so . . . ethereal. It felt safer in the computer, floating around in there in bytes and RAMs or whatever they're called. There was something about having a hard copy that scared me. Printing it out made it *real*—being able to hold it in my hand, knowing that anyone could just pick it up and start reading it and maybe criticize it, judge it. . . . It would be so vulnerable."

She shook her head. "God, that sounds so stupid now."

"No, it doesn't," Tanner said gently. "Go on. Please. I want to hear this."

Kat let out another breath. "I called it *The View from Here*. I think it was good—very good, maybe. But it wasn't very commercial. I knew that even while I was writing it. I knew no publisher would take on something like it from a writer who had never published a book. I thought that getting *something* published might make it possible, give me some credibility."

"Enter the Janssens," Tanner surmised.

"Right on cue," Kat said with a grimly ironic smile. "Winslow got a hot tip on them and wanted to commission an entire book based on it, a juicy tell-all with a bombshell ending. My agent got me the contract." She shook her head. "Only my grand plan turned out to be all for nothing."

"Why?"

"It was on the laptop, *The View from Here*—" She had to stop as the tears she'd been fighting surged up, and she couldn't hold back a sudden sob. "The virus . . . It's gone," she finally managed, finishing in a whisper.

Tanner reached over to the side table and pulled a tissue from the box and handed it to her. "I'm so sorry, Kat," he said softly.

"Me too," Kat said, smiling a little. "Now it's like I've sold my soul for nothing."

"That's a little dramatic, isn't it?"

Kat gave him a halfhearted shrug. "It's how I feel."

"So what was it about? Your novel?" Tanner asked after a moment. "If you don't mind talking about it."

"I don't," Kat said, and she thought for a long moment. She'd never told anyone about the book, and it was strange trying to find words for concepts so very familiar to her.

As Kat formulated her thoughts, Tanner took a lock of her hair and twirled it around his fingers. It was a small gesture, but Kat was touched by the innocent intimacy of it.

"It's about a woman, an orphan," she finally began, "who is desperately afraid of feeling again the loneliness she felt as a child. She moves to New York to surround herself with as many people as possible, literally. She takes classes, joins a health club, volunteers for all sort of things, basically doing everything possible to make as many friends as she can. And for a while it works. In the end, though, well, she ends up realizing she *is* alone after all, in a fundamental way. The only person she can truly count on is herself.

"It's really about that, I guess, how we're *all* fundamentally alone, no matter how many people we stack up around us to ward it off. You come into the world a lone being, and that's how you leave it. Pretending anything else in the interim is just a fantasy, a fallacy, fake.

It doesn't matter how much you love them—friends, family—or how much they love you. They can still be gone in a heartbeat, and then you're alone. That's when true loneliness sets in, because you realize what's missing."

Beside her, Tanner listened, but Kat was barely aware of him now, so intent was she on getting her thoughts out in the right words. "People go through life thinking they're protected from that feeling, but there's an ax hanging over them the whole time, and they don't even know it. They think they're safe, but they're not. I guess my book is—was—about exposing that truth."

Kat rested her head against the sofa and let out a long breath, then glanced over at Tanner to gauge his reaction. He was nodding contemplatively. "So," he began, extending the word, "maybe Tennyson had it wrong? Maybe it *isn't* better to have loved and lost? Maybe it *is* better never to have loved at all?"

"Exactly," Kat said, glad he'd understood.

Tanner stared up at the red-splashed ceiling, his eyebrows furrowed as he considered what she'd said. Finally he turned to look at her. "Is that why your phone never rings?"

His question was so unexpected, so jarring, it took a moment for the words to sink in. "My phone rings," Kat protested, then immediately cringed at the defensiveness in her tone.

"Besides Winslow," Tanner said, his tone and expression not challenging, only . . . intent.

"I don't have time for a lot of friends," Kat said, and now her voice had a whiny tinge to it. "I'm a writer," she argued to his annoyingly patient silence. How did they get on this track anyway? "It's a lonely business," she ended lamely.

"Maybe that's why you chose it," Tanner suggested. "I mean, you spent all that time—ten years—*alone,* writing a book on how wonderful it is not to be lonely. But were you really so happy all that time?"

"Oh, just forget it," Kat grumbled, turning her back to him and picking up one of the small sofa pillows. She yanked on several loose threads dangling from the seams. "You wouldn't understand."

"Oh, no?" Tanner said gently, and Kat felt the sofa cushion beneath her shift as Tanner moved closer to her. "I'm not letting you run away from this." He put his hand on her arm, but she shrugged it off.

Tanner let out a loud breath. "Look, Kat, I don't mean to sound condescending or preachy. . . . I just can't stand the thought of you living your life like that, afraid to get close to anyone out of fear you'll eventually lose them. Or, worse, your ending up with Winslow, which amounts to the same thing. You don't love him."

At that, Kat drew in a harsh breath, furious, and spun around to glare at him. "Oh, really? How do you know that? What do you know about love anyway? You and your 'one thing' policy."

But Tanner didn't answer right away. Instead he only explored her face for a long moment before laying his head against the back of the sofa, his gaze shifting again to the ceiling. "You know, we've had these kids up to the ranch a few times." Kat let out a breath. Again, his words were so unexpected, so seemingly out of context, she could only wait impatiently for him to get to the blasted point.

"Sick kids from Denver Children's Hospital, some terminal. You should see these kids." He glanced over at Kat, then returned his gaze to the ceiling, shaking his head in amazement. "People don't think they understand what's happening to them, but they do. And they don't hold back for one minute, not one second. They fully embrace the life they have left, however short it may be."

He laughed lightly. "From the moment they arrive at the ranch, they fall in love with everything—the mountains, the horses, the staff. Tillie, our cook, is so great with them. . . ." Kat frowned. Had his voice broken just a little on that last word? Yes, it had, she realized, seeing a tear make its way down Tanner's cheek, gleaming wet and red in the neon light from the Danforth.

Tanner brushed it away and turned to face her, his eyes locking on hers. "If your parents knew the pain their dying would cause you, would they have loved you any less to ease it? Or Andrea?" Now Kat felt tears swimming in her own eyes. "And would you have loved them any less to lessen your pain now?" Kat's tears spilled out as she shook her head, unable to speak.

"Of course not," Tanner said softly, moving closer to

her. "You can't think that way. That's not living." He gave her a sad grin as he smoothed a strand of hair off her wet cheeks. After a moment he began again, his voice barely a whisper but thick with emotion. "Please, Kat, you have to take love wherever you can get it, grab it, snatch it up when it's offered, cherish it precisely *because* you don't know how long it will last."

Kat looked at him, his face blurry through her tears, yet she could see the expression in his eyes, so earnest, so imploring, so . . . loving? Yes, there was no other explanation for that intensity. She knew it in that instant. After all his "one thing" rhetoric, he *was* offering his love to her.

And maybe he was right. Maybe it was time to let down her guard, her defenses, fully embrace life as those children did, allow herself to love and be loved— by this man sitting next to her.

She gave him a small, hesitant smile. "Thank you." Seeing his surprised expression, Kat realized it may have been an odd thing to say, but it seemed somehow appropriate to her.

Tanner smiled, seeming to understand. "You're welcome."

And then a thick wave of exhaustion came over Kat, physical but also emotional, yet she welcomed it. An unfamiliar peace had come right along with it, wrapping around her body, soft and warm.

"I'd better get some sleep," she said, smiling. "I have a lot of packing to do tomorrow."

They rose from the sofa, and Tanner walked her to her bedroom door. He looked into her eyes for a long moment, then leaned in to kiss her cheek, his lips lingering there, then sliding back, his breath warm on her ear. "Good night, Miss Callahan."

He pulled back and smiled once more at her, sweet and tender. But just as he turned away to head for his own room, Kat caught something else in his eyes. Sadness? No. Resignation. What about? Being beaten at his own "one thing" game? Well, too bad!

Once she was alone, Kat changed into her pajamas, brushed her teeth, and washed her face, humming all the while. But as she was patting her face dry with a towel, she remembered. She was leaving for the ranch the day after tomorrow. Only one more day with him. No, she needed more than that, needed to see where this was going, explore it. Never before had she felt this way, and she wasn't going to let him get away.

And then it came to her, and she smiled at her reflection in the mirror. The perfect solution.

In his room, Luke stared up at the ceiling, sleep the last thing on his mind. He couldn't stop thinking about Kat—the scent of her hair, her skin, the feel of her lips against his, the love shining in her large brown eyes. This was no longer about Kat the writer, was it? It was all about the woman now.

Just a few weeks ago he'd been prepared to—no, *planned* to—use whatever romantic feelings he could generate against her to stop the book—whatever it took. And after tonight he knew he'd succeeded in at least that part of it. She was in love with him. He'd seen it in her eyes, tasted it on her lips.

Unfortunately, he'd fallen just as hard. No way could he use what was now between them in this nasty business.

Thank God he'd taken care of that last batch of DNA. He'd had to do it himself this time, since he fired that idiot private eye. The tech at the lab must have seen the desperation in his eyes, judging from the amount he'd demanded. Of course he'd gotten it. Luke would have paid anything he asked for.

It was, after all, their one and only safety net—flimsy as it was. And it bought him some time. Time to figure out how to make this right.

Chapter Sixteen

Kat awoke to the sound of a soft rap on her bedroom door. She blinked against a ray of sunlight coming in through the slats of the blinds. Glancing at the bedside clock, Kat's eyes widened when she saw the time. It was the middle of the afternoon!

"Hey, sleepyhead, you awake in there?"

Kat looked into the full-length mirror across the room on her bathroom door and cringed at her messy hair. She combed it quickly with her fingers.

"Yes, come in!"

Freshly shaved and dressed in those familiar jeans and a bright white T-shirt, Tanner walked in carrying two steaming mugs of coffee, the scent of cinnamon wafting through the room. "Good morning—or should I say afternoon?"

"Afternoon, I guess," Kat said, taking one of the mugs. "Thanks. But why did you let me sleep so long?"

He shrugged. "You needed it. You've been working really hard the last few days. And we were up pretty late last night. Don't worry, I'll help you pack."

He looked around the small room for somewhere to sit, but there were no chairs. Only the bed. Kat was surprised to feel a wave of shyness course through her. Nodding down at the bed, she murmured, "There's fine."

She was surprised to see a shy cast in his eyes too as he sat down. He occupied himself by blowing across the top of the hot mug.

Okay, now or never.

"I—I want to ask you something."

"Hmm?" And suddenly Kat felt nervous and awkward, like a girl on Sadie Hawkins Day about to ask a boy to dance for the first time.

"Well, you know I'm leaving for the ranch tomorrow. . . ."

"Yes?" he asked, a slightly bemused smile playing on his lips.

"And, well, I thought maybe you could—" But the shrill ring of the phone on the nightstand interrupted her.

"I guess you'd better hold that thought."

Kat nodded and picked up the phone from the nightstand. "See?" she whispered, smiling in self-satisfaction. "My phone rings." But then she put the phone to her ear. "Oh, hi, Brian," she said, grinning as Tanner raised his eyebrows in an I-told-you-so.

"What's up?" Kat said into the phone, turning away from Tanner so she could concentrate on the call.

"We got some news from the first lab," Brian answered, his tone gruff, although Kat detected an edge of excitement in it. "They said the material had been 'compromised.' No shocker there."

"Again?" Kat groaned. Behind her, she heard Tanner blow across the top of his coffee. "What about the other lab?"

At that moment, Tanner burst out into a racking cough. He must have choked on the hot coffee. She turned to see him putting the mug down on the floor, one hand pressed against his chest as he coughed.

"Is that the cowboy?" Brian was asking in that unpleasant, snide tone of his. "What, did he take too big a bite of his afternoon T-bone?"

Ignoring him, Kat turned to look at Tanner, becoming concerned as his coughing continued unabated.

"Hold on," she said perfunctorily into the phone, then set it down on the nightstand as she stood up. She headed into the kitchen, poured a glass of water, and rushed back into the room. Thankfully, Tanner was breathing more easily. Still, he took a sip of the water and several deep breaths.

"Sorry," he said in a raspy voice. He waved at the phone. "Go on. I'm fine."

Kat picked it up. "Okay, I'm back. You were saying about the other lab's results . . . ?"

"You'd better get down here," Brian said by way of an answer. "There've been some . . . developments."

"Right, right, nothing over the phone," Kat grumbled, remembering the mandate from Upstairs. God, they were paranoid. She actually didn't even care about the results anymore—or the book itself, for that matter. She *did,* though, want to talk to Brian about their relationship before she left for Colorado the next day—with Tanner in tow, she hoped. She wouldn't feel right about any of this until she did. "I'll be there in a half hour."

Leaning across the bed to hang up the phone, Kat sighed. "I have to go down to—" She stopped when she saw Tanner's face, his eyes. It looked as if someone had just punched him in the stomach. He was visibly pale, every muscle in his body tensed.

"Are you okay?" Kat asked, putting a hand on his leg. He didn't seem to notice, staring down blankly at the rug on the floor. "Tanner?" Kat leaned closer, trying to make eye contact with him. She squeezed his leg harder. "Tanner!"

"What?" he said automatically, blinking as if just waking up. "Oh. Sorry. I'm fine." He glanced up at her, and she frowned when she saw his eyes again. His confidence, self-assuredness, had vanished, replaced by something she hadn't seen before—utter defeat. And misery.

Seeing his helpless gaze fall back to the floor, Kat wished she didn't have to go. She wanted to get to the bottom of this.

"Look," she began, her voice firm, "I've got to go down to Winslow for a while."

Now Tanner raised his shoulders in one quick, impatient shrug. "So, go." Taken aback by his dismissive, irritated tone, Kat only looked at him with absolutely no clue what to say or do. Tanner felt her stare and raised his head to look at her, a harsh scowl on his face. "What? I said I'm fine. Go if you're going."

Kat touched his forearm gently, baffled. Why was he acting like this? "Tanner—" She stopped when he visibly flinched at her touch and stood up quickly.

"Really, Kat, stop." His voice, so gruff, so annoyed, made her wince. Finally he looked directly at her, and now she wished he hadn't, the look in his eyes fierce, angry, desperate—an entire range of emotions, and she didn't understand any of them. Not one.

He sighed deeply. "I'm tired, Kat, that's all. I just want to lie down for a while. Is that all right with you? I didn't sleep all day like you did, remember?"

Kat's jaw clenched hard at his accusing tone. "Fine," she said in a low voice. "If that's the way you want it, fine."

He nodded once, curt and hard, then left the room.

Her hands curling into fists at her sides, Kat strode into her bathroom and slammed the door shut, the mirror on the back of it knocking against the wood.

She looked at her reflection over the sink, saw the hurt, the bewilderment in her eyes. She'd allowed Tanner McIntyre into her heart, let down her defenses to him, and now it was too late to erect them again. A moment later she saw a hard edge forming in her eyes as the pendulum swung back. Anger was good.

Oh, but who was she kidding? The damage had been done. "Jerk," she mumbled, yanking aside the shower curtain.

Despite her anger, though, before she even turned on the water, her face was already wet with warm, salty tears.

When he heard the hair dryer go on in the other room, Luke reached over, opened the drawer of the nightstand, and pulled out his cell phone. Letting out a breath, he pushed the speed dial button.

"It's me," he said grimly into the phone when she answered.

"What's wrong?" she asked, her tone instantly matching his.

"They used two labs this time. We only knew about the one."

"Oh, Luke." Her voice sounded so uncharacteristically small and weak, it nearly broke his heart. He felt in that instant that he'd failed her miserably.

"Damn him!" Luke slammed his fist down on the bed. "That idiotic buffoon. How did he miss that? Tracking the DNA was supposed to be priority number one."

She was quiet for a moment, then asked, "What are we going to do, Luke?" God, her tone—so helpless, so frightened—flew in the face of the strong, independent woman he loved so very much. He wished he could tell her that everything would be all right. But he didn't know that, did he? Not anymore. Nothing was certain anymore.

Damn, he'd been *counting* on that information about the lab's being accurate. At last he let out a long, ragged breath in resignation. No use crying over spilled milk. What was done was done. Luke's shoulders sagged as he let go of his anger, the reality of the situation sinking in fast.

"What else *can* we do? There's no time for anything else. We have to tell her the truth. All of it. Now." The silence on the other end spoke volumes. "I know"—he acknowledged the unstated concern—"the ever-malleable truth."

"Do you think she can actually help us?" she asked softly, hope, however tentative, seeping in through the words.

Luke let out a mirthless chuckle. "Maybe. She's been getting pretty darn cozy with the Winslow clan lately."

"All right, then, do it. It seems we have no choice." Her voice sounded more resolved now, more like *her.* That was good.

"I'll take her to Josephine's," Luke said, thinking out loud. "In such an elegant place she may be less apt to throw her linguini into my lap once she knows the truth."

"Oh, come on, honey," she said, laughing despite the gravity of their situation. "Turn on some of that famous 'McIntyre' charm!"

"Gets 'em every time," Luke quipped. God, it was good to hear the sound of her laugh. It had been far too rare a sound over the last several months.

Shaking her head, her jaw tight, Kat turned off the hair dryer and grabbed her brush. After all he'd said to her the night before, the tender way he'd kissed her, so gentle and sweet, could she have been wrong?

Her stomach tightened as she tugged her brush through a tangle in her hair. Maybe he hadn't meant *his* love when he'd told her to be open to it, but just love in general? No. It wasn't all in her mind. She'd been right about Tanner last night. She *had.*

Maybe he was just as afraid of his feelings as she had been—for different reasons probably, although she couldn't fathom what they might be. Maybe he'd kept to his "one thing" policy as a way of distancing himself from real love. But why? Did something happen to him in the past to make him shy away from intimacy? Yes, something was going on with him, and she was going to find out what that was.

It was his own fault after all. He'd forced open her heart, pried apart its rusty hinges, given her a taste of what she'd been missing all this time, and she'd fight for that now.

She would lay out her feelings to him, tell him how much she cared about him. She had to take the chance, no matter the outcome.

Determined, Kat set her brush down beside the sink

and headed toward his room but stopped at the threshold when she heard Tanner's voice. "Either way you're going to have to leave the ranch." He was sitting on the bed, talking on his cell phone, his back to her.

Kat felt guilty listening to his private conversation but couldn't make herself walk away.

"Go to the house in Bali," he was saying into the phone, his voice tense and urgent, "tonight if you can. The heat's going to turn way up now and—" The person he was talking to had apparently interrupted him—and with bad news, Kat guessed, seeing Tanner rake his free hand through his hair in agitation. "Can't be moved at all? Are you sure?"

At that moment he seemed to sense Kat behind him, and he glanced over his shoulder at her. He looked startled. "Oh, hi." Kat frowned. Was his tone a shade too casual? And was that guilt hovering in his eyes?

Then she heard a tinny voice coming from the phone. A woman? Tanner listened for a moment, then nodded. "Okay, I'll call you later. Bye."

He hung up the phone and put it down on the pillow.

Think fast, Luke told himself as he turned around to face Kat. How much had she heard? He'd been listening for the hair dryer to turn off but had become too involved in the conversation, especially when he learned there'd been a turn for the worse.

Kat looked embarrassed, a blush coloring the tops of her cheekbones. "I'm sorry, I didn't mean to eavesdrop."

Luke shrugged off her apology. "That was my sister." It was the only logical thing he could think of to say.

"Is everything all right?" Kat asked, her lovely red-tinged eyebrows furrowed in concern. Hell, he couldn't wait to come clean with her, no matter the outcome. But not here, not now. She was in a hurry to get to the Winslow building, and he wanted to take his time with it. Besides, there were far too many potentially lethal projectiles within reach.

"Oh, she's fine," he answered dismissively.

"Good." But then confusion crept into her eyes. "I thought she lived in Albuquerque, she and her husband."

So, she'd heard the part about the ranch. "Oh, they do," Luke said quickly, his mind whirring. And then inspiration struck. It was flimsy, but it would have to do, for the time being anyway. And what was one more lie after so many?

"They came to the ranch for a surprise visit before they left for their time-share in Bali. I guess they forgot I was going to be here in New York." He was getting into the rhythm of the lie now. It was frightening how adept he'd become at it.

"She was calling to let me know that the boiler in my cabin broke this morning. It started overheating. They turned it off, but it's still too hot to be moved right now, so it won't be replaced until tomorrow. It's going to be cold tonight, so I told her they should leave for their vacation tonight." Luke stopped and held his breath. He thought the feeble story covered everything she may have overheard, but would she buy it?

"Oh," was all Kat said, frowning slightly as she incorporated the story.

Maybe he wasn't such a good liar after all. It had sounded good in his head, but out loud it seemed contrived and convoluted to him. Still, it had been the best he could do under the circumstances.

"But it'll be fixed by the time I get there, right?" Kat asked.

Luke nodded. "Absolutely."

"Okay," she said with a light shrug. "Too bad they missed you."

Luke forced a sigh and nodded. "I'll have to go out and see them sometime in Albuquerque." There. That was the last lie he would ever tell her. It would probably also be his last opportunity. There was a very good chance she'd never want to see him again after he told her the truth.

No, he told himself, *think positively.*

To that end, he stood and walked over to her. He smiled into her deep brown eyes but cringed inwardly when he saw the wariness in them. He couldn't blame her, though. "Look, I'm sorry about blowing up before, really. I'd like to make it up to you. How about Josephine's—that place you've always wanted to try—for dinner? My treat."

"Oh, you don't have to do that," Kat said, shaking her head adamantly. "It's much too expens—"

But Luke stopped her by pressing his fingertips against her lips. He took a step closer to her. "I want to," he said softly. "Besides, there's something I want to tell you, about why I acted like that."

Kat nodded. "There's something I want to tell you too." Her eyes darted away from his, and color again splashed her wonderfully freckled cheeks.

"Good, then it's settled. I'll make reservations for six-thirty. Is that enough time?"

"It should be," Kat said, nodding. "I'll have to meet you there, though." Worry flashed in her eyes. "Oh, but is this nice enough for Josephine's?" She looked down at what she was wearing, a simple but elegant dark green pantsuit that perfectly complemented the fiery colors in her hair.

"Mmm," Luke purred, smiling as he cupped her face in his hands. "You're breathtaking." He caressed her lips with his thumbs before leaning in to kiss her, perhaps for the last time. He made it count, savoring her soft, full lips under his, committing the feel of them to memory.

Finally, reluctantly, he released her and watched her walk away from him. Hearing the front door close behind her, Luke chuckled wryly to himself as he glanced over at his closet, his eyes passing over the two suits he'd brought with him. "I wonder which one'll go better with linguini."

Chapter Seventeen

Brian slid the manila envelope across the desk toward Kat, then sat back in his chair, his arms folded across his chest, a self-satisfied smile on his lips.

Kat picked up the envelope and pulled out the bound report. She flipped through it, her eyes scanning the colorful graphs, complex tables, numerical probabilities, and heaven knew what else. In the back were several sheets of DNA graphs.

Kat shrugged and laid the report on her lap. "So what's it all mean?"

Brian grinned, every bit the cat who ate the canary. Irritated, Kat sighed. At this point she just wanted him to get on with it so they could have the conversation she'd really come here to have.

Already he'd kept her waiting for more than an hour,

darting in and out of his office, tossing "Just a sec, hon's" over his shoulder. Through the open door, Kat could hear the entire office buzzing. What was going on? She'd been about to go out and grab someone to ask when Brian finally came in and closed the door, test results in hand.

He sat forward in his chair, his hands clasped together, his eyes shining with excitement. Kat saw his knuckles whiten as he nodded down at the report. "How much do you know about DNA testing?"

"Not a lot," Kat said perfunctorily. She also didn't understand his dramatic tone. What was the big deal? Either Jeremy was Alex's son or not, right?

"Neither did I. But I've learned quite a bit today. Now, on something they call a four-probe test, the samples were consistent with what we've been hearing all these years—that Alex Janssen really *is* Jeremy's father."

Kat frowned but nodded. Even though she had no idea what a four-probe test was, she knew that wasn't the end of the story. If that result were true, she'd have spent the last year writing a tell-all book with nothing to tell—not to mention the thousands of dollars Winslow had already spent on the marketing campaign. And Brian would certainly not be sitting there fidgeting with barely concealed glee. But if he dragged out the dramatic pause for one more second, she was going to scream.

"That's not all, though," he said quickly, wisely sensing her impatience. "They went deeper, Kat, did more tests. And those results showed several fine discrepancies. . . ." Again he stopped for effect, obviously—and annoyingly—loving every moment of this.

"Brian . . ." Kat said, her tone warning.

"It's not Alex," Brian said simply, but his brown eyes gleamed. "It's got to be a close relative, though. Very close. A brother. And he's only got one . . ."

"Luke," Kat whispered. "Wow." So Luke Janssen was Jeremy's real father. Kat sat back in her chair, dumbfounded, her eyes staring down at what amounted to a true bombshell lying on her lap.

"What we have on him is pretty sketchy," Brian was saying, his tone more matter-of-fact as he sat back in his chair. "We're all scrambling now, playing catch-up. I was hoping you would know more about him, maybe have more information in your notes than you included in the book?"

Kat thought for a moment, then shrugged. "I don't know, Brian. He's an elusive guy, and I frankly didn't spend a lot of time on him. He's pretty boring, actually—some kind of software developer. I didn't think he was very relevant. I mean, he and Alex haven't even talked for years."

"Well, we're still trying to track him down." Brian shrugged as if there wasn't much hope. "He's a wily one. We don't have one decent picture of him. His former secretary said he was camera shy to the extreme. His picture's not even in his own corporate brochure."

Kat nodded, racking her memory for any further bits of information. "I remember that his wife died."

Brian nodded. "More than ten years ago. During premature labor. The kid died too. After that, ol' Luke pretty much fell off the radar."

"Even from his own brother."

Brian snorted unpleasantly. "Well, apparently the estrangement didn't include Victoria Janssen."

But Kat only shuddered. It all suddenly made her skin crawl. All of it. The lies, the phony, media-hyped images . . . At that moment Kat realized she felt strangely betrayed by the Janssens.

As she'd been writing the book, she'd developed something of an affection for Alex and Victoria Janssen. They'd seemed so devoted to each other through the years, as truly in love as any couple she'd ever seen, including her mother and father. Maybe that was the source of her feelings for them—they reminded her of her parents. Kat shook her head and was surprised to find tears welling in her eyes. Blinking them away, she took a deep breath and sat up straighter.

No, she wanted nothing more to do with the Janssens or their sordid sexual history. She wanted to concentrate on her *own* life. She wanted to tell Tanner how she felt and see if he'd consider shortening his stay here to spend time with her in Colorado. Maybe she'd even start working on a new novel while she was there.

"This is all we have on him," Brian was saying as he

slid a file across the desk. "I made you a copy so you could get started on the rewrite of the final chapter."

Kat had picked up the file automatically but dropped it back down onto the desk now as if it were suddenly coated with poison. "Can't someone else do it?"

Brian's eyebrows dipped in confusion. "Don't you want to? Put the icing on the cake, as it were?"

But Kat shook her head resolutely. "Really, Brian, I don't. At this point a Martian could have fathered the kid, and I still wouldn't want to do it. It all seems so sordid to me now." She let out a mirthless chuckle. "Trashy."

Brian sat back in his chair and studied her for a long moment. Finally he shrugged. "I guess we could put something together. Actually, maybe I'll do it myself. It might be kind of fun. As long as you're sure?"

Kat nodded. "Absolutely."

"All right, then." His voice became more tender as he continued. "I guess I was hoping you'd pass on Colorado, stay here to write it." He stood up, came around the desk, and sat down in the chair across from her. "I'm really going to miss you, Kat."

He took her hands and leaned in for a kiss, but Kat drew back. "Actually, Brian, there's something else I wanted to talk to you about."

"Oh?" Brian's smile faltered as if he'd already sensed what she was going to say. "Okay." He looked at his watch. "How about over dinner? I'm starving."

"Oh, no!" Kat exclaimed, looking at her own watch.

"I have to go. I'm sorry." She stood up. "Can we talk tomorrow morning, though? Before I leave?"

Brian looked a little nonplussed, and Kat knew he was wondering where she was going in such a hurry, whom she was going to meet. He had to suspect already.

"Okay, sure," he said a shade too breezily as he stood up.

"Oh, you don't have to walk me out," Kat said quickly, leaning over to collect her purse from beside the chair. "I know you're busy with all this. I'll just come by on my way to the airport tomorrow, all right?"

"Sure," Brian said as she headed for the door. "And, Kat?"

Kat stopped, let out a breath, and turned around slowly. She knew from his tone what he was about to say.

"Yes?" she asked, her light tone every bit as forced as his had been.

Brian stepped closer to her, and for a moment his brown eyes searched hers, looking for assurances Kat knew he wouldn't find. "Never mind. I guess I'll just see you tomorrow, then." Kat winced inwardly when she saw that the smile on his lips wasn't in the least bit reflected in his eyes.

Her stomach tight with guilt and sadness, she nodded and walked out the door. She didn't want to hurt Brian and knew she was doing exactly that.

Still, she had to follow her heart, and right now it led her to only one place—Josephine's—where even now Tanner probably sat waiting for her.

Chapter Eighteen

Seated across from Tanner amid the understated elegance of Josephine's, Kat had a hard time taking her eyes off him.

He looked absolutely stunning in a dark gray suit, crisp white shirt, and a blue silk tie that set off his eyes brilliantly. She hadn't even known he'd brought a suit to New York with him, but there he'd been, sitting alone as he waited for her, seemingly perfectly at ease in the exclusive restaurant, surrounded by the Who's Who of New York City.

In fact, seeing him calmly sipping Pellegrino water from an exquisite crystal glass, Kat found it difficult to believe this man spent his life rustling cattle up and down muddy fields.

Despite obvious effort, though, he hadn't quite been

able to tame his wild curls. Several rogue strands sticking out every which way clashed charmingly with the elegant neatness of the suit.

"Mmm, that was wonderful," she said, laying her fork down on her empty plate. She'd ordered salmon Wellington and had enjoyed every bite, the fresh fish tender and flaky, the pastry shell crisp and buttery.

Tanner had opted for veal picatta, the house specialty, and he nodded in agreement as he took his last bite.

When the waiter came by a moment later to take away their plates, they waved away the dessert menu but ordered two cappuccinos.

While waiting for their coffee, they sat in what Kat felt was an expectant silence, both thinking of what they wanted to say to each other. By the time the waiter came back to set the steaming cups in front of them, Kat felt ready.

Okay, she thought, stirring the frothy milk down into the pungent coffee, *it's time.* She drew in a deep breath. "Look, Tanner, I know we've only known—"

But Tanner had spoken at the same time. "Before I say what I have to say—"

They stopped and laughed lightly, but it sounded nervous and awkward from them both.

"You first," Kat said, grateful for the reprieve.

Tanner nodded, reached across the table, and took her hand, holding it in both of his. He looked at her intently, and Kat was surprised to see fear hovering in his eyes. "No matter what happens from this point on, I just want you to know that I've enjoyed every minute I've had with you. I think you're a fascinating, complex woman, and more than anything else in the world I'd like to . . ."

But Kat was having a hard time concentrating on his words, distracted by a woman she saw in her peripheral vision; she somehow knew that the woman was blatantly staring at their table from across the room. Finally, unable to suppress her curiosity, Kat glanced at the woman directly and swallowed hard when she recognized her.

"Oh, my," she whispered to Tanner while keeping her eyes on the woman. "It's Jessica Beaumont! And she's staring right at us!"

During the research phase of her book, Kat had tried to contact Jessica Beaumont numerous times. The two-time Academy Award winner had been Victoria Janssen's best friend for years. She'd only been able to get through to one of the star's many reps, though, who said he'd give Ms. Beaumont the messages. Kat had never heard from her.

As she now watched breathlessly, Jessica Beaumont stood up, excusing herself from her companion—a much younger man with movie-star good looks, although Kat didn't think she'd seen him before.

"I think she's coming over here!"

The star was indeed making her way across the room in all her elegant drama. Her chin lifted regally, she flung her long white scarf back over one shoulder, aware all eyes were on her.

"She must think we're somebody!" Kat whispered,

her heart beating fast. She kept thinking that the woman would stop and turn around as soon as she realized her mistake, but she didn't. She came directly to their table and placed one hand possessively on the edge of it, her aquiline nose high in the air as if deeply affronted.

Close up, Kat thought her even more stunning than on-screen. Although well into her forties—no one knew exactly just *how* far—Jessica Beaumont easily could have passed for early thirties, with the substantial surgical help she readily admitted to.

Now she was giving Tanner a piercing look with her dark gray eyes. "My, my, my," she began, dragging out each word in her slow southern drawl. "Look who's here, one of my oldest and dearest friends—or so I thought."

Pulling her hand up off the table, she planted it on one slender hip and turned her eyes to Kat, her tone confiding, "Now really, I would think a *real* friend, a *true* friend would call an old pal when he's in town, wouldn't you?"

After an excruciating moment of silence, Kat realized that a response was expected. "Yes, yes, of course," she said, her voice strained and hoarse.

Ms. Beaumont nodded in satisfaction. "See?" She turned back to Tanner, and only then did Kat get a good look at him, her attention before riveted on Ms. Beaumont.

Kat had thought Tanner looked pale after his coughing fit earlier, but now he was positively ashen except for bright red splotches across his cheekbones. He was staring down at the salt and pepper shakers on the table, a deer-in-the-headlights expression on his face.

"All right, I forgive you," Ms. Beaumont said despite his silence. Her lips broke out into a wide smile, her teeth brilliant and white against scarlet lipstick, her signature color. "Now come on, sugar, let me see that handsome mug of yours."

Placing her index finger delicately under Tanner's chin, she raised his head. For a moment he glanced miserably at Kat, seemingly desperate to communicate something to her with his eyes. His lips moved soundlessly, and Kat thought she saw him mouth *I'm sorry* before raising his eyes to Ms. Beaumont's.

"Luke, Luke, Luke," Ms. Beaumont said, shaking her head, "it's *so* good to see you. You and your friend here simply *must* come and visit me in my cozy little place in the Hamptons. . . ."

But Kat was no longer listening. *Luke?* Jessica Beaumont had called Tanner *Luke*?

As it suddenly clicked into place in Kat's mind, the room seemed to fall away from her, becoming distant, all the sounds in the restaurant muffled by the rushing blood in her ears. She was having a hard time breathing too, her lungs seemingly shrunken to half their size. Her stomach lurched. Oh, no, she was going to . . .

"Excuse me," she muttered as she stood up, almost tripping over the chair. Averting her eyes from them, she made her way to the restroom, her legs wobbly and unreliable beneath her.

"Kat!" she heard from behind her. It was Tanner—no, not Tanner but Luke. Luke Janssen. Kat shook her head, trying to shake the haze that had suddenly engulfed her brain. Was this really happening?

Kat ignored him, all her energy focused on getting to the restroom where, she hoped, the world would slow down for one damn minute and let her think, figure it all out, find out the answers to the million questions suddenly bombarding her brain.

"My, my, my," Jessica Beaumont purred, her eyes on Kat as she disappeared into the ladies' room. "Was it something I said?"

Seeing her flutter her eyelashes in that coy way of hers, Luke rolled his eyes. "All right, Jessie, you can drop the act." His voice was stern, but he couldn't suppress an affectionate smile at his old friend as he leaned in to kiss her cheek. "We both know you grew up one bridge over in Brooklyn," he whispered into her ear.

"Why, sugar, I simply have no idea what you're talking about!" Jessica did her eyelash thing again as she settled herself in Kat's vacated seat. "So, tell me, Luke, wherever did you find her?" She gave an indistinct wave toward the restroom. "She's lovely by the way, just lovely. And that hair . . ." Clucking admiringly, she turned her gray eyes back to Luke, her eyebrows furrowed in exaggerated concern. "I do hope I didn't ruin things for you."

Luke sighed. "No, you're fine. You just rushed it a little." Quickly he explained the situation to her. Just as he was finishing, his cell phone rang. His stomach tightened as he read the caller ID screen before flipping open the phone.

As he listened intently for the next thirty seconds or so, his face grew serious. "I'm on my way," he said curtly, then hung up. He put the phone back into his pocket, stood, and pulled out his wallet. "I have to get out there," he said as he counted out some bills and threw them onto the table. "Hey, Jess, do me a favor, will you?"

"Name it," Jessica said simply, rising from her seat.

Luke glanced over at the restroom. If only he had more time . . . But it was too late now. Much too late.

Kat splashed some cold water onto her face, welcoming the harsh sting of it. She stared at herself in the mirror, watching the water drip off her chin as she shook her head.

"How could you have been so stupid?" she muttered to her reflection. "So naïve? So easily duped?" Thankfully, she was alone in the ornate marble bathroom. She picked up one of the plush hand towels from the counter and dabbed her face with it.

One thing was certain: Upstairs at Winslow had been right to be so paranoid. And she'd played right into their hands, hadn't she, whoever was behind it all—Luke and Victoria Janssen probably and possibly Alex. Did he know about their affair? Or that Jeremy wasn't his biological son?

Either way, she'd let Luke Janssen walk right into her

own house, let him spy on her, use her. Kat let out a breath and turned away from the mirror, disgusted with herself. She leaned against the counter, her hands folded across her chest.

" 'Tanner McIntyre,' " she mumbled, shaking her head, the big, tough cowboy from Colorado on his "first visit" to the big city. Right. Luke Janssen had lived in New York for how many years?

Snippets of their conversations replayed in her mind, the sympathetic, understanding way he'd talked to her about her family, how she'd poured her soul out to him as she'd never done with anyone else. And what had she gotten in return? Bald-faced lies!

No, the "cowboy" was really just a glorified computer nerd, wasn't he? He'd probably sent that e-mail himself, the one containing the "rad" virus Benny had mooned over. Hell, Luke Janssen probably designed the blasted thing himself. And it had certainly been effective, hadn't it? Destroying ten painful years of effort. Damn him!

Tears stung in her eyes, but she blinked hard against them. She wouldn't give him the satisfaction.

So what else had they done to stop the book? Of course, she realized, the difficulties with the DNA—not only in obtaining the samples but sabotaging what little material Winslow *had* gotten hold of. The various DNA techs had obviously been well paid to compromise or conveniently misplace the samples. Cold, hard cash certainly went a long way, didn't it? But not far enough, Kat thought with satisfaction. Ultimately Winslow had gotten the results they'd needed, hadn't they? From the second lab!

Kat spun around to face herself in the mirror, her eyes opened wide. Luke Janssen hadn't known about the second lab! She'd mentioned it while on the phone with Brian, and he'd immediately broken into that coughing fit! And no wonder he'd had such a violent reaction. He knew it was a done deal at that point, the DNA results the last hurdle before Winslow published the book.

She would have to rethink everything now. What was true, what was a lie? For one thing, was there even a ranch out there in Colorado, or was that all part of the ruse?

Oh, but he'd mentioned the ranch, hadn't he, during the phone call she'd overheard that morning between him and his sister. Kat took in a sharp breath. " 'Sister,' my—" she muttered but stopped as a tall brunet came into the restroom. She gave Kat an odd look before heading into one of the stalls. Kat didn't care.

Yes, they'd been talking about the ranch before he'd known she was listening. So it had to be real. Wow. For months the entire world had been clamoring for news on the Janssens' whereabouts, and she, Kat Callahan, knew exactly where they were—well, Victoria anyway.

But for how long? Her eyebrows furrowed, Kat tried to remember the rest of the phone call. Luke had been urging Victoria to leave the ranch, but there'd been some kind of problem, something that was delaying her.

As the other woman came out of the stall and washed

her hands, she gave Kat another strange look before leaving. Kat knew she had to go back to the table, back to Luke Janssen. But what would she say to him? What would he say to her?

Her heart racing, Kat exited the restroom, and, taking a deep breath, she turned the corner to their table.

Luke Janssen was gone. Their waiter was walking away, counting a small stack of cash as a busboy cleared away their coffee cups.

"Coward," she muttered under her breath. Glancing across the restaurant, Kat saw that Jessica Beaumont and her young companion had also left.

As Kat pulled her suit jacket from the back of her chair and put it on, she thought about what to do now. Brian. She had to tell him about this. As she pulled her cell phone from her purse and flipped it open, she realized that her jaw was clenched so hard, it hurt.

The feeling of betrayal she'd had before was quickly escalating into outright fury. This was personal now. Luke Janssen had used her, made her have feelings for him—all to protect his lover's secret.

Well, two could play that little game. He'd invaded her territory under false pretenses, barged in on her life and turned it upside-down. Now it was her turn. And she knew just where to go for some answers. It would serve them right for the truth—the *whole* truth— to come out. And she'd be the one to do it!

Consciously relaxing her jaw, Kat pressed the speed dial button for Brian. "It's me," she said when he picked up. "Better stop the proverbial presses. It seems our friendly neighborhood cowboy was none other than Luke Janssen in the flesh, out to sabotage the book."

"My God, Kat."

"Yep. Apparently acting runs strong in that family. Look, Brian, I have to get out there, to the ranch. ASAP. I think they're there, the Janssens."

"Take the Lear. I'll have it ready to go at La Guardia in an hour." His voice was a little shaky and breathless. "You think Luke's on his way to the ranch too?"

"Maybe." But then another thought struck her. There was no way he had faked his love for Lucy. "He does have to pick up his dog first, though."

"I'm already in the limo," Brian said, his voice suddenly urgent. "I'll meet you there."

Kat agreed and hung up the phone. Heading for the door, she realized she had no idea what she would say to Luke Janssen if he *was* back at her condo. She suspected that her first impulse would be to slap him across the face, hard—give him a taste of the pain he'd caused her.

"Here, let me," Brian said, and Kat gratefully handed him the key to the front door. He'd always had better luck with the lock. After only a few seconds of jiggling, Brian got the door open, and they rushed inside and across the lobby.

Mrs. Burgstrom was waiting by the elevator, accompanied by another older woman Kat knew was part of Mrs. Burgstrom's tea entourage. The woman lived on the second floor, and Kat didn't want to waste time with the extra stop.

"The stairs," she mumbled to Brian, already on her way to the door to the stairwell. They took the steps two at a time, and Kat was breathless by the time she reached the third floor.

When she opened her door, only Oliver came out to greet her. No Lucy. "He's gone."

Brian let out a frustrated breath. "Well, let's check inside just in case." He didn't sound hopeful.

Just as Kat was about to follow Brian inside, Jackie's door opened. "Hey, Kat."

"Hi, Jackie," Kat said distractedly, glancing over at her. She frowned, seeing how drained Jackie looked behind her thick makeup. The effect made her face look even more masklike than usual.

"Are you all right?" Kat asked.

Jackie nodded slowly as if she weren't completely sure. "Jessica Beaumont was just here," she said in a disbelieving tone. "*The* Jessica Beaumont. She went into your place and came out with Lucy." Her eyes finally focused on Kat. "Do you *know* her?"

Kat let out a mirthless chuckle. "Apparently she's an old pal of our friend 'Tanner.'"

"Oh," Jackie said, still looking a little dazed. As she turned to go back into her condo, Brian came out of Kat's, shaking his head. "He's not here." He gave her a pragmatic shrug. "All right, you'd better get to the airport. I'll take Oliver until you get back."

"Thanks," Kat said, heading inside. She went into her room and changed into jeans, a sweatshirt, and boots. Not knowing how the next few hours would pan out, she grabbed her toothbrush and another change of clothes and threw them into her grandmother's old valise. "You take the limo," Brian said once they were back outside. "I'll get a cab." He opened the limo door for her.

Just as Kat was about to climb in, Brian stopped her with a light touch on her arm. "And, hey, Kat?" he began, his voice soft. Kat turned back to him. "I'm sorry he hurt you." Brian's tone, so sweet, so sympathetic, sliced right through Kat's armor of anger, leaving her heart exposed, vulnerable. Tears welled up in her eyes as only now did the real pain and betrayal begin to settle in.

"Oh, sweetheart," Brian said, pulling her into his arms. He hugged her for a long moment, not with the passion of a lover but with the tenderness of a friend. "Take care of yourself out there," he whispered into her ear.

Kat could no longer speak and so only nodded. She wiped away the first wave of tears as she climbed into the limo. When the driver saw her face in the rearview mirror, he tactfully raised the barrier to the back, leaving Kat alone in her misery.

Chapter Nineteen

Kat yawned and blinked, trying not to become hypnotized by the steady blips of yellow from the center line of the road shining in her headlights. Thank God for caffeine. She could feel it bravely battling back the relentless onslaught of sleepiness.

She'd tried to nap on the plane, but her thoughts kept racing, oscillating between anger and hurt, until it felt as if two permanent grooves had been dug into her mind, becoming trenches by the time they'd landed at the small Aspen airport.

Now, an hour later, she was driving through yet another small town—really just two blocks of a main street. If not for the Taco Bell on one corner, the town could have been a set for a western movie with its quaint

Victorian houses and storefront facades, all only dimly lit by a couple of streetlights set far apart.

Driving through the sleeping town, Kat felt as if she were the only awake person on the planet. And so very alone. A moment later, though, the now-familiar rage returned. She would never have felt this way if *he* hadn't made her open herself up to him. Life on her own had been just fine, thank you very much, regardless of Tennyson's little theory. She slapped her palm hard against the steering wheel. "Jerk!"

Gritting her teeth, she stepped on the gas pedal. She wanted this over with now so she could go back to New York and try to reclaim her old life.

A couple of miles past that last town, Kat turned off the main road onto a smaller one that supposedly led to the ranch, based on the map Luke Janssen had sent her when they'd made arrangements for the vacation swap— back when she thought she was dealing with a simple ranch foreman named Tanner McIntyre. Now she had no way of knowing if it was even a real map.

But then she saw it, up ahead to the left, a large square arch made of thick logs. That had to be the entrance to the ranch, assuming the map was indeed accurate.

As she drove up and stopped in front of it, she saw SHALLOW J splayed out in block letters across the top of the arch. This was definitely the place.

Driving under the arch, she found herself on a gravel road, the tires crunching in the quiet night. She drove on for about a half mile through a forest of aspens, the trees rising, delicate and slender, from either side of the road. Rolling down the window, she drew in a breath of the fresh, cool night air. How she wished the circumstances of this visit were different.

Finally, after one last hairpin turn, she saw up ahead a three-story, century-old farmhouse set off by a long driveway. A wraparound porch encircled the front half of the house, several Adirondack chairs clumped in the corners. On her map of the ranch it was marked *Main House.*

An Audi, a Porsche Boxter, and a Mercedes SUV were parked in the semicircle drive in front of the house, a good sign that Victoria Janssen was still here. A year earlier Kat had seen a picture of Victoria getting out of a similar SUV in *Juicy Weekly.*

Kat stopped just before the turn-off to the driveway and watched the house for a moment, unsure how to proceed. Lights blazed from several of the rooms on the second floor, so it seemed probable someone was awake.

A shadow moved in the window above the front door, and Kat's throat went dry. Was she being watched? Had some electronic gizmo alerted whoever was in the house to her presence? She had no idea what her welcome—or lack thereof—would be. But what did it matter anyway?

She had every right to be here. She'd made the vacation swap in good faith. *They'd* created this situation, not her. But what would she say to them? She'd been so caught up in her whirling emotions, she hadn't thought any of this through. There were just too many un-knowns. Was Victoria even here? Were she and Luke still lovers? And what about Alex Janssen? Did he know about them? Did he know that Jeremy wasn't his son? And where was he now? Or Jeremy?

Finally Kat let out a frustrated breath and turned the ignition off right where she was. There wasn't room enough to park in front of the house anyway, and she needed to get this over with. Now. Her plan was simple: confront whoever was inside that house and demand an explanation. She definitely deserved it, the way they'd used her, manipulated her life.

Resolved, Kat got out of the car and slammed the door shut, not caring who heard it.

Immediately she was struck by the odd quality of light surrounding her. She looked up, and her eyes widened at the brilliant display of stars overhead, entire new layers of them she'd never seen before. They looked much closer than they did in New York, and she smiled as she realized she'd actually taken a step back, as if they'd been about to come right down on top of her.

In the sky to the left Orion towered over her, resplendent and powerful as he pulled back on his massive bow. And there was the Big Dipper, although a large cloud hid its smaller companion. "My God," Kat whispered as she realized that that was no cloud.

It was a mountain, soaring high above the ranch, the magnificent, snow-covered summit gleaming gray-white in the starlight. The spectacular sight before her blurred as unexpected tears filled Kat's eyes. She closed her eyes against them and after a moment became aware of the extraordinary quiet of the place. Keeping her eyes closed, she just listened for a minute.

But it wasn't quiet after all, was it? There *were* sounds here, just very different from the noises of the city. In fact, it sounded remarkably similar to the CD Tanner had played the night of her birthday, complete with a babbling creek running along the other side of the road.

Opening her eyes, she looked over there and saw a wooden footbridge spanning the creek. Beyond that was a fenced-in pasture, the dewdrops in the grass glittering like diamonds in the light mist hovering close to the ground.

At the sound of a horse whinnying, Kat took in a quick, excited breath and peered out farther into the pasture. Her heart swelled when she saw four horses out there—two dark ones, a white one, and a palomino—all standing still and strong like sentinels, the mist swirling around their hooves.

As she watched, the palomino shook its head, whinnying, its thick mane flying loose around its shoulders. Could it be Pepperjack, the "ace galloper"? But then she let out a scoffing breath. There she went, making assumptions again. Did Pepperjack even exist? Or was he just another one of Luke Janssen's many lies?

It was time to sort the truth from the lies. Yes, this

"city girl" was about to get some answers out here in the middle of the country.

Fueled by renewed anger, Kat headed straight for the house. She walked up the semicircular driveway and past the cars, not minding the crunch of her footfalls on the gravel, not caring if anyone knew she was coming or not.

She paused at the bottom of the stairs leading up to the porch, listening for any sounds coming from inside the house, but she heard nothing. What would she do if they simply didn't answer the door? Would she really just barge right in? *Yes,* she decided, setting her jaw. At that moment she felt justified in doing anything.

The shadow moved again in the room above the front door. *Okay,* she thought, *now or never.* Swallowing hard, Kat climbed the stairs and walked up to the door, the heels of her shoes clacking loudly on the wooden porch.

Taking a deep breath, Kat lifted her hand to ring the bell but froze as an earsplitting shriek sliced through the air. *What the—* The scream came again, sustained now. She looked up to the window where the shadow had been. Someone was in terrible agony in there! She had to do something.

Frantic, Kat grabbed the doorknob with both hands and turned it, holding her breath. She let it out in a gush of air as the knob turned in her grasp, unlocked.

Flinging open the door, she rushed inside and scrambled up the staircase, nearly tripping halfway up. At the top she stopped, breathing hard as she looked down a long hallway filled with closed doors, desperately trying to orient herself. Finally she ran to the one she guessed opened to the room above the front door.

Her heart thudding in her chest, Kat turned the doorknob and swung open the door. "Hello? Are you all ri—" The words died in her throat as she got a look inside the room, her eyes widening as she took in the hospital bed next to the window, a child lying nestled in the thick covers.

Kat recognized him immediately: Jeremy Janssen— or, rather the ghost of him, his face pale and gaunt under a Lakers cap that nearly overwhelmed his small features. Tears gleamed wet on his closed eyelids.

He was more than just pale, though, Kat saw as she approached the bed. A network of thin blue veins crisscrossed beneath the nearly translucent skin of his cheeks. In stark contrast, the spaces around his eyes were dark and shadowy. The combined effect gave his face an almost skull-like appearance. Kat could also see by the outline of the covers how dangerously thin he'd become.

The bed was surrounded by medical equipment, some of which Kat recognized from her grandmother's hospital stays: an EKG machine, a blood pressure monitor, another machine she didn't recognize pumping dark crimson blood through a tube inserted into the boy's arm. A steady beep kept time to his heartbeat. If not for that sound, she wouldn't have been surprised if the child were—

"Hi, who are you?".

Kat looked back at Jeremy's face, his eyes open now and trained on her. His voice sounded so weak, so strained. . . . His eyes, though, the same intense green as his mother's, were like two beacons of light amid the pallor and shadows surrounding them.

"I'm Jeremy," he said, each syllable a struggle. Instinctively Kat stepped closer so he wouldn't have to work so hard to be heard. "Everyone calls me Jiminy, though, 'cuz I liked Jiminy Cricket so much when I was little. Do you like him?"

Numb, Kat nodded, her mind trying to absorb the sight of the gravely ill child before her, so different from the robust little boy smiling out so happily from the pages of *Life* two years before. The magazine had done a five-page layout of the "First Family of Hollywood," as it had proclaimed the Janssens.

"Good." His eyebrows furrowed then, and Kat was struck by the similarity to Tanner's—no, *Luke's*—expression of confusion, the brows identical in shape. "So why are you here anyway? I don't get too many visitors."

"I heard a scream," Kat explained around a lump that had formed in her throat.

Jeremy's confused expression melted into a sheepish, embarrassed grin. "Oh, that was just me. It's the shot in my back. That's how I get my medicine." His small features tightened. "I hate those. Probably I should be used to them by now, but I'm not. Have you ever had a shot like that?"

Kat nodded, wincing as she remembered the spinal tap she'd endured as a teenager when she'd had a high fever and the doctor suspected meningitis. The thought of such a frail child having to withstand a shot like that— and frequently, apparently—made the lump in her throat thicken and tears well in her eyes. That long, thick needle . . . And for him to scream like that when he could barely talk, the pain must have been excruciating. Clearly it had wiped him out.

"I'm so sorry," she said, her voice choking up. She blinked back tears, but one escaped, and she brushed it quickly away, feeling a sudden need to be strong in front of this sick child.

"Oh, it's okay," Jeremy said, shrugging his bone-thin shoulders under the sheet. "I get a milkshake when it's done—'if I'm up to it.'" Kat couldn't suppress a smile at the adult inflection he'd put into his tone for the last few words. "My mom's getting—"

"Who the hell are you, and what are you doing in here?" Startled, Kat turned toward a connecting door in the room, where a gray-haired man wearing a mask, green scrubs, and a stethoscope stood, his ice blue eyes boring into hers. "You can't be in here without a mask and gown. Do you have any idea of the risk of infect—"

"It's okay, Dr. Phelps," another voice said from behind Kat. A familiar voice. Kat turned around slowly.

And there she was. Victoria Janssen was standing at the door to the room, holding a glass with a straw in it. She, too, wore green scrubs over her clothes and a mask covering her nose and mouth. But there were those eyes, those famous catlike eyes, radiating a gentle, maternal kindness. Something else lurked in the brilliant green of them, though, something Kat hadn't seen in any of her many films—fear, deeply entrenched.

"Ms. Callahan, I presume?" Victoria Janssen asked, her eyebrows raised above the mask.

Speechless, Kat only nodded.

"Luke said you might pay us a visit. I assume you have some questions for me?"

Surprised, Kat nodded again and suddenly felt like one of those silly bobble-head toys.

"Uh, let's see, Alex is asleep in our room. . . . Why don't you wait in the room across the hall? That's Luke's, but he's out seeing to a sick foal right now. I'll be right in after I give his highness here his beloved milkshake."

Her gaze turned toward the bed, and Kat could almost physically feel the love, the adoration, flowing from Victoria's eyes as she looked at her son. She moved toward the bed, and Kat shook her head dazedly, trying to soak it all in. Even though she'd been fully expecting to see her, Kat still found it hard to believe that the world-famous movie star was right there in front of her.

But then she saw the woman's signature walk, her hips swaying back and forth provocatively, still outrageously sexy even after so many years. Millions of women had tried to imitate it. Kat herself had attempted it a time or two, but she'd come nowhere close.

Dr. Phelps cleared his throat, harsh and loud, wrenching Kat from her reverie. He was standing by the bed, his hands on his hips, glaring first at her, then the door, mentally shoving her out.

"Sorry," Kat mumbled before walking quickly out of the room.

Chapter Twenty

The moment she walked into the room across the hall, Kat knew it was Luke Janssen's room. His smell permeated the air. Just the scent of him sent another wave of emotions swirling through her, emotions she couldn't deal with right now. Shaking them out of her head, she walked across the room to an overstuffed chair by the window. She took off her jacket, laid it over the back of the chair, and sat down.

It was a large room, tastefully decorated in the rich masculine colors of burgundy and navy. A suitcase lay open on the bedspread, the gray suit he'd worn to Josephine's flung carelessly across the top.

Kat leaned back in the chair and closed her eyes, trying to get a handle on her thoughts before Victoria Janssen came in. At least now she knew the other Janssens were

218

definitely here at the ranch. But were Victoria and Alex still together? Evidently. Victoria had said "our room."

So that much she knew. Immediately, though, the same questions she'd been grappling with for hours resurfaced. Did Alex know about Victoria's affair with his brother? Did he know that Jeremy wasn't his biological son? Is that what all this was about? Keeping the truth from him?

Kat hoped she would get some straight answers. A moment ago Victoria had seemed amenable to talking to her. At least she hadn't thrown Kat out on her ear. Yet.

"Try to get some sleep, okay?" Kat heard from the other room. "I love you, sweetheart."

The other door clicked shut, and Kat stood up as Victoria Janssen came into the room, reaching up to untie the mask. She then shrugged out of the scrubs, revealing a tailored white shirt, slightly wrinkled. She also wore fitted gray slacks, although both the shirt and slacks looked too large for her. The woman had definitely lost weight since the last photograph Kat had seen of her.

Despite her weight loss, though, Victoria was still stunning, even without an ounce of makeup. Like Jessica Beaumont, she appeared years younger than her age but without the too-taut smoothness of plastic surgery.

Victoria nodded down at Kat's chair. "Sit, please. Can I get you anything?"

Kat only shook her head as she sat back down, not yet finding her voice, a little intimidated by being in the same room with the world-famous movie star.

"Fine, then," Victoria said, moving the suitcase back as she sat down at the foot of the bed. She steepled her fingers and gave Kat a frank look, finding and holding her eyes. "Look, Ms. Callahan—"

" 'Kat,' please," Kat said automatically, but she was glad she'd at least managed to say *something*.

"All right, Kat. And I'm Victoria—or Vic, if that's too much of a mouthful. I never cared for 'Vickie.' I always thought it a bit too peppy for me." She smiled at Kat then, and the natural warmth of it made it easy to see why all of America—the *world*—had loved her for so many years.

Kat realized then that her anger had dissipated quite a bit in the last few minutes, but it wasn't gone completely. It was more . . . on hold. Thinking of the child in the other room, she decided to at least hear the woman out.

Victoria drew in a deep breath and let it out. "As you can see, Kat, my son is very sick. He has acute lymphocytic leukemia."

"I'm sorry," Kat said, and she immediately felt the inadequacy of the words. "He—he looks so weak."

Victoria nodded. "He is." Tears glistened in her cat-like eyes, but she blinked them back and continued. "We had quite a scare earlier. Jeremy's cancer treatments led to a recent bout of blood poisoning, and because of that he went into anaphylactic shock tonight. It was touch-and-go there for a while."

Reliving what must have been a horrific few hours, Victoria blinked back more tears, but this time she wasn't fast enough, and a stream of them trickled down each of her too-thin cheeks.

Tears welling in her own eyes, Kat stood, walked to the nightstand, and grabbed a box of tissues. Taking one, she handed the box to Victoria, who nodded her thanks. As Victoria wiped her eyes, Kat thought about asking if Jeremy was okay now, but it was painfully clear that the child was still a very long way from okay.

Unexpectedly Victoria sprang up off the bed and began pacing up and down alongside it, rubbing her palms together. Stopping in front of the bed, she gave Kat an ironic smile, and Kat caught a glimpse of dazzling white teeth, perfect except for the front left one, turned slightly—and famously—inward. "Hell, I can't believe I'm about to tell the most intimate details of our lives to a reporter."

Kat winced at the bitter edge to the woman's voice. "Oh, but I'm not a report—" she began automatically, but she stopped midword. After all, writing a tell-all book was really no different from any of those gossip rags like *Juicy Weekly,* was it? Perhaps even worse. A tinge of shame crept deeply into her chest.

"Luke says we can trust you, though," Victoria was saying, "so here goes." She sat back down on the bed and gave a light shrug. "I guess I'll just start at the beginning." Leaning forward, she rested her elbows on her knees, clasped her hands together, and looked at Kat, resolve strengthening her gaze.

"Well, for years Alex and I put off starting a family,

our careers the number-one priority. We were so caught up in the struggle of it at first, and then, as we began to get bigger and better roles, the fame and money took over, and of course there was the artistic satisfaction. It was all so . . . addictive. But as the years went on, I became increasingly unfulfilled by it all. Something was missing. . . ."

"A child," Kat prompted.

Victoria nodded and gave Kat a wry smile. "You can't exactly cradle an Oscar in your arms, nurture it, watch it grow and thrive." Her smile faltered, and Kat understood that the woman was thinking of Jeremy, of perhaps not getting the chance to see him reach adulthood.

Victoria let out a breath before continuing. "Anyway, after a year with no success, we went to a fertility doctor, a Dr. Eugene Carr." A dark look passed through her green eyes at the mention of the doctor's name. "The 'best in the business,' we were told. He did some tests and found that Alex had too low a sperm count for us to conceive." She let out a gush of air. "Obviously, we were upset and began going over our options."

Kat sat up straighter as she realized where this was heading. "Luke," she said matter-of-factly, and Victoria nodded.

"You have to understand that all of this was happening during the time that Luke was . . . well, for years he'd distanced himself from us—ostracized himself, really." She drew in a long breath and let it out. "You see, after Luke moved out here from New York, he married a wonderful woman named Annie. They lived in Denver, in a renovated loft downtown. God, they were so happy together—so young, so in love." She shook her head, smiling sadly as she remembered.

"They both worked night and day getting Luke's company off the ground," Victoria continued. "They poured all their youthful energy into it." She let out a little laugh. "Well, not *all* of it, I guess. Just when the company was really taking off, Annie found out she was pregnant. They were ecstatic. We all were. I'd just wrapped up *The Viennese Lover* and had some time before my next film. I flew out to help paint the nursery and decorate it— Beatrix Potter characters everywhere."

Victoria's smile faded again, and she brought her arms up across her chest, hugging herself. "But, as I'm sure you know from your research, Annie went into labor far too early and started hemorrhaging uncontrollably after giving birth to their little boy." Her gaze fell to the rug in front of her. "The baby's lungs weren't developed enough, and he died after only a few minutes. I got to see him, though."

She looked back up at Kat through teary eyes. "He was so tiny, that baby, he could have fit in my hand." Victoria pulled another tissue out of the box and dabbed at her wet cheeks. "After Annie died, Luke pulled away from us, their friends, everyone." She brought her hands together, interlacing her fingers. "He threw himself into his company, working twelve-, fourteen-hour days but not with the passion and enthusiasm of before—more out of desperation, needing to focus on something to keep his mind from the pain he never really let himself feel."

She gathered her hands into tight fists and squeezed them hard, her knuckles whitening. "We tried so hard to bring him back to us. We'd come through Denver whenever we could, but Luke would always avoid spending any real time with us. We called him every week, every Sunday night, but most of the time he wouldn't even answer the phone. The times he did, though, were even harder to take. He sounded so . . . empty.

"He'd only talk about his company, the new branch offices he'd opened, the number of employees, the projects he was working on. Never anything about his feelings and *absolutely* nothing about Annie or the baby. If we even came close to talking about them, he'd just about hang up on us and then not answer his phone for weeks afterward. It was like he was disconnected from . . . well, himself, from life, not just from us."

She sat up straighter then, crossing her legs. "Just about the time we found out about our fertility problem, I began to sense a shift in Luke. Nothing dramatic—he still didn't want to talk about Annie or his feelings— but . . . I don't know, after talking to us for a while, he just didn't seem to want to hang up.

"So when we found out about Alex, we immediately thought of Luke—the chance at a baby, of course, but we also thought it might help bring him back to us. I flew out from LA to talk to him about it, and well . . ."

"Best decision I ever made," a soft voice said from the doorway.

Kat looked up to see Luke Janssen standing there, the knees of his Levi's caked with dried mud, a streak of it on his cheek. Kat inhaled sharply, her stomach doing flip-flops at the mere sight of him. Luckily, Lucy came bounding into the room, a perfect distraction.

"Hey, girl," Kat said as the dog came over to her, her tail wagging hard. The fur on her left side was matted with mud, so Kat patted the Lab's other side, desperately trying to calm the butterflies suddenly swarming in her stomach.

"Easiest one too," Luke continued as he strode to the bed and sat down next to Victoria. He put an arm around her waist and kissed her cheek with brotherly affection. Victoria reached over to brush the dirt off his face with her thumb.

Glancing up from Lucy, Kat couldn't help but notice a natural affinity between Luke and Victoria, not romantic in the least, more . . . supportive.

"How's the foal?" Victoria asked.

Luke gave a light shrug. "If he makes it through the night, he should be all right."

Lucy went to Luke and laid down in front of him. Luke's gaze turned to Kat, his lips curling up into a hesitant smile, but Kat couldn't return it. The pain was too sharp, too stabbing, too deep. She was beginning to understand why they'd done all this, but that didn't excuse him from playing with her mind, her heart. Kat felt her jaw clench tightly, her eyes hardening, and took some satisfaction in seeing Luke wince as if she'd slapped him.

He sighed, squeezed Victoria's waist, and stood up. "Well, I guess I'll leave you two to talk. I'm going to go check on the Cricket. Lucy, you stay here, girl." The Lab slapped her tail against the floor.

Victoria watched Luke leave, a fond smile on her lips. "He's a good man, Kat, a wonderful man, like his brother."

Kat said nothing, her jaw still set.

Victoria let out a breath. "Okay, so where was I? Oh, yes. So when I came out to talk to Luke, he finally broke down and cried in front of me. We talked all night—about Annie, the baby, his feelings of hopelessness, the vast void he felt in his heart, his soul. By morning, he'd agreed to go to counseling. It really helped him too. Obviously, there will always be pain there, but he's no longer so terribly crippled by it."

She leaned back on the bed, supporting herself with her hands. "As for us, Alex and I were thrilled, both at the possibility of a baby but also at having Luke back in our little fold—which quickly expanded, and on the first try." Her eyes darted to the room across the hall to her son, a small, intense smile on her lips.

But Kat frowned, her brows furrowed, as she thought back to what she knew about this family. "But I thought Alex and Luke were still estranged, even now."

Victoria nodded. "We kept it quiet, Luke's being part

of the family again, because he was so fiercely private. He hated—no, *abhorred*—having his name or picture in the papers or on TV for everyone to gawk at. So he stayed away from us in public, which was fine with us. We had him back in our lives, and that's all that mattered.

"But, backing up a little, when we went to Dr. Carr with—" she stopped, letting out a little chuckle—"the 'goods,' as it were, we didn't tell him who the source was, although obviously he knew it wasn't Alex."

She sat up again and clenched her hands together, her knuckles again whitening. "A couple of years ago, though, dear Dr. Carr paid us a little visit. Apparently he'd been spending quite a bit of time in Las Vegas and had lost a good deal of money out there, got in over his head. . . ."

"He blackmailed you?"

Victoria nodded, her mouth a tight slit, her eyes cold. "He knew the situation, knew the truth, knew I didn't cheat on Alex, yet he said he could make it sound cheap and sordid, implying . . . well, the obvious."

"Couldn't you have gone to the police?"

Victoria shrugged. "I don't know, maybe. We weren't exactly thinking clearly. See, this all happened just as Jeremy was getting sick. Our focus was on him, one hundred percent. And so we paid Carr off, really just to make him go away."

"But he didn't," Kat guessed.

Her jaw rigid with anger, Victoria shook her head.

"He came to us every couple of months, and we kept paying him—an absurd amount of money, really, but that was the least of our concerns." Her eyebrows came together in a scowl. "And then the snake sold the story to Winslow anyway, despite our paying him."

Kat winced at the fury in the woman's eyes, even though she knew it wasn't directed at her—although maybe she deserved some of it. She was no innocent in this, was she?

"Anyway, our lawyer didn't think there was much of a chance of stopping the book through legal channels— the story's basically true after all. Luke *is* Jeremy's biological father. And we can't exactly prove we *didn't* have an affair. Besides that, the publicity of a lawsuit would only increase sales when the book did come out." Her eyes fell to the bedspread beside her, and she began fingering a small thread sticking up out of it. "And so, purely out of desperation, when we got your e-mails and phone calls, knew you were writing the book, we began to . . . take steps."

"Enter 'Tanner McIntyre,'" Kat said, her jaw set.

Victoria nodded and looked back over at Kat in that frank, open way of hers. "I'm sorry, Kat. I'm sorry we deceived you. You have to understand, though, *he* was our motivation." Her eyes flicked over to the room across the hall. "Our *sole* motivation. It was never about our careers or our images. It was always about him."

She sat back again, propping herself up with her hands. "See, Jeremy loves the Internet. It's his window to a world he can't participate in right now. He spends *hours* on that thing, his laptop." She gave Kat a small, proud smile. "He's great with computers, just like his Uncle Luke."

At that, Kat raised her eyebrows inquisitively.

"No, Jeremy doesn't know." Victoria answered the unspoken question. "We were actually about to tell him when he got sick." She shrugged. "After that, it just didn't seem so important anymore. Besides, we weren't sure how he'd take it, and the doctor said to keep stress to a minimum." Her face tightened around a wry chuckle. "Talk about stress. We knew that once the book came out, the story would be all over the Internet. Can you imagine the headlines?"

A shudder vibrated across Victoria's thin shoulders, and she looked away from Kat, as if the mere sight of her sickened her. Kat suddenly felt about an inch tall. The thought that she'd caused this family more grief than they already had weighed heavily on her mind. She realized, too, that she was now firmly on their side in this, when only minutes before she'd been furious with them. The jury, however, was still very much out on how she felt about *Luke* Janssen.

"I've seen the ugly side of fame, Kat," Victoria was saying, "*lived* it—the lack of privacy, forever dodging the paparazzi in their relentless quest for the money shot." She shrugged pragmatically. "But, really, who can blame them? They're just part of a huge, greedy machine. People love to see the big downfall. They're hungry for it, almost like a bloodlust. And Alex and I were ripe for it, the downfall—overdue, in fact."

As if on cue, Alex Janssen walked in, yawning and stretching his arms out over his head. His short, dark hair, usually so perfectly coiffed in all his films, stuck straight up on one side. He wore jeans and a wrinkled black T-shirt he'd obviously slept in.

"Hey, hon'," Victoria said, smiling up at him. "This is Kat Callahan."

"Ah, the archenemy," Alex said with a light chuckle as he walked toward Kat. "Nice to meet you. I'm Alex." As he shook her hand, his lips curled up into that half grin of his that made millions of women forget all about their husbands or boyfriends for the duration of it. "Funny, you don't look all that dangerous."

His brown eyes gleamed, so similar to his brother's except for the color and the way they turned up at the corners, whereas Luke's were more down-turned. *Ah,* Kat thought, that was what she'd thought was somehow "wrong" when she first met "Tanner," what seemed like a million years—a million *emotions*—before. She wished now that she'd pursued that thought, made the connection between the two brothers. It would have saved her a lot of heartache.

Alex sat down next to his wife and took her hand. Bringing it up to his lips, he kissed the inside of her wrist, closing his eyes as if relishing her, even after so many years.

But Victoria was giving him an amused, sidelong smile. "You look just like Alfalfa from the Little Rascals!" She reached up and gently patted down his hair, though most of it sprang right back up.

As his wife groomed him, Alex gave Kat an aw-shucks look and again he reminded her of "Tanner"—their first few moments together. She drew in a deep breath and let it out slowly. She had to stop thinking that way.

Giving up on Alex's hair, Victoria turned her gaze back to Kat. "Yep, this guy here and I have made it through a lot of years together, our marriage surviving far longer than is customary in Hollywood."

"How dare we!" Alex said with a wink at Kat, and she couldn't help smiling back at him. Clearly, his famous charm wasn't just written into in his movie scripts.

Watching the two stars banter back and forth, Kat realized she *had* been right about them. The deep love and respect glowed strong and vibrantly between them, almost tangible in its intensity.

And, despite the fact that they were both Academy Award-winning actors, Kat's instincts told her they weren't acting now. She believed them, every word.

"Of course," Victoria continued, "we had a blip or two on the downfall meter. All in all, though, we fared pretty well through the years. And then we had our Jeremy." She smiled, but the expression faded as she let out a worried breath. Obviously sensing his wife's thoughts, Alex squeezed her hand.

Kat was thinking over what she'd been told. "Why didn't you just tell me all of this from the start? I would have written the book differently."

"Well, Kat," Alex began slowly after a solemn glance at his wife, "it's been our experience that most of the time people aren't really interested in the truth, especially when there's money involved. We've learned that the hard way, multiple times."

Victoria nodded. "That's why we don't do personal interviews anymore. Our words kept being taken out of context or creatively edited to get whatever slant they were after. We had no control over it."

Kat thought about that but shook her head. "But I *was* interested in the truth. That's why I e-mailed you and called so many times. I *wanted* the truth."

Alex gave her an even look. "Maybe *you* did, Kat, but would Winslow have published the truth? Would the real story have sold as many books as a titillating account of a sleazy affair between Victoria and my brother?"

Kat shrugged. "I don't know, maybe."

"We've been betrayed by more reporters than I care to remember. They're after a story, and they'll do whatever they deem necessary to get it, even if it hurts people." Alex trained a direct gaze on Kat, and she saw no trace of his levity from just a few moments earlier. "And this time it's about our son, Kat. Our *son*."

Victoria let out a deep breath. "And Winslow's the worst of them all. They're like vultures—more dangerous than the paparazzi because they're not out in the open. Greedy executives hiding behind thick board-room doors, distancing themselves by printing their trash through imprints, shielding their pristine reputations while destroying everyone else's."

Again Kat cringed at the fury in Victoria's voice. She'd had dinner with those "greedy executives" just the night before! Heck, Brian was *one* of them. And then she remembered how eager they'd all been about the book. The word *blood lust* was not far off the mark. Maybe they *would* have slanted the story in the most titillating way they could in order to sell more books.

"All right, Pilgrim." Kat heard Luke's bad imitation of John Wayne from the other room. "Hold on to them thar horses."

A moment later Luke appeared in the doorway, pulling his mask down and reaching back to untie his scrubs. "He can't sleep," he told Alex and Victoria. "He wants his mom and dad."

They both nodded and stood up. Victoria picked up her mask and gown but then turned back to Kat. "I'm really sorry you were caught in the middle of all this. And I do believe you would have tried to help us. I just don't think it would have done any good."

As Victoria let out a deep sigh, Kat realized the woman had already resigned herself to Winslow's publishing the book with the sleazy-affair angle. Kat wasn't willing to throw in the towel quite yet, though. During the last few minutes an idea had begun forming in her mind, a possible solution to this mess.

"Luke told us why you agreed to write the book," Victoria continued, "to get your first novel published. I hope that works out for you."

Alex nodded, his mouth grim. "At least something good would come out of it."

Victoria touched Kat's forearm then, her eyes sympathetic. "He told us what happened to your family too. I'm so very sorry."

"Thank you," Kat said, forcing a smile, but it disappeared the moment they turned away. How dare Luke tell them that, something she'd told "Tanner" in confidence?

But then the pendulum came swinging right back at her. Who was she to be so outraged by an invasion of privacy? She'd spent months snooping around, prying into the lives of these people. Still, that realization did nothing to assuage her anger. In fact, irrational as it was, being reminded of her guilt, her own culpability in all this, only fanned the flames of it.

Chapter Twenty-one

"Mind if I come in?" Luke asked, his tone tentative. He was still standing by the door, his mask and gown now draped over his arm.

"It's *your* room," Kat muttered, willing herself to get up, to walk out of there, get someplace where she could think through the details of her idea. It involved staying on longer here, but she thought she could handle it as long as she kept contact with this man to a minimum.

"I'm sorry I ran out of Josephine's like that," Luke said, tossing his mask and gown onto the bed before sitting down across from her. "Vic called about Jeremy's going into shock, and I had to get out here."

Kat nodded but didn't say anything, not trusting her voice. She couldn't even look at him right then. Instead, she turned to face the window. Outside, a band of glowing light came from the east as the sun rose.

Kat heard the bed creak, and out of the corner of her eye she saw Luke lean toward her, his hands raised in supplication.

"Look, Kat, I'm sorry I lied to you. I hated doing it. I was actually going to tell you the truth at Josephine's."

At this, Kat felt a wave of renewed anger wash over her, and she turned to look at him through narrowed eyes. "Of course you were. You were out of options, so you decided to play your trump card—*me*. Use how I felt about you, how you'd *made* me feel about you, to manipulate me into helping you." Suddenly unable to bear the sight of him, she looked back outside.

"It wasn't like that, Kat, not at all." She heard him let out a frustrated breath. "All right, maybe it was at first. But then it all changed." Then, softer, he pleaded, "Will you look at me, please?"

Her jaw set, Kat turned to him, giving him a steely look.

"You have to understand, I'd do anything for them, Kat. Anything. Vic and Alex helped me through the most difficult time of my life. They were really there for me, even when—*especially* when—I tried my best to push them away. That's why I understood so well how you felt—your isolation, your loneliness."

Again Kat bristled, giving him a resolute nod. "Oh, yes, you knew *exactly* how I felt. And you used it to make me care about you, to make me—" No, she wasn't going to say *those* words. "You said all the right things, pushed the right buttons—all so calculated and deliberate."

Luke let out a long breath, his shoulders lowering. "I'm sorry, Kat. I'm so sorry." He chuckled then, dry and mirthless. "You know, I wasn't even going to get so involved at first. When they asked for my help, I intended only to hire a private investigator—"

At this, Kat raised her eyebrows in surprise. "That man! The one following me?"

"Yes," Luke answered, his mouth forming a tight line. "I hired him to follow you, track the progress of the book, look for ways to stop it or at least delay it." He let out a contemptuous breath. "One of my cows could have done a better job than he did. When I realized he wasn't providing me with enough useful information, I took another tack. I went on the Internet and pulled up everything you'd ever written."

"Looking for an 'in'?" Kat asked sardonically.

"Well, yes," Luke admitted with a small shrug. "It was the article you wrote for *Dog's Life* I found the most interesting. You mentioned a ranch as a possible vacation destination for dog owners, and something in the way you described it—I don't know, longingly, I guess—told me that was my 'in.' So I took a chance, even though I knew it was a long shot. I registered on the site under the name of my real ranch manager, Tanner McIntyre, described the Shallow J, and—"

"And I fell for it, hook et al. What an idiot."

Luke made a frustrated noise deep in his throat as he

leaned forward, his palms raised. "Please, Kat, try to under—"

"Oh, but I *do,*" Kat interrupted, the words crisp. "I do understand. And you know what? You might even get what you wanted from me after all. I *am* going to help—or try to anyway. I have an idea that might work. I have to talk to Brian first, work out the details. Is there somewhere I can go?"

Luke nodded. "The cabin. Tanner's in Albuquerque visiting Luanne."

Kat raised her eyebrows. "So the cabin's real?"

"Of course. Everything I told you about this place was real."

Kat couldn't stifle an ironic snort. "Not everything, 'Tanner.'" She sat up straighter and looked at Luke squarely. "I want you to understand something. I'm doing this for that sick little kid in there and his parents, not *you*. And once it's done, I'm leaving here, and I never want to see you again."

She stood, grabbed her jacket, and headed for the door, but Luke reached over and grabbed her hand as she passed him. "Please, Kat, don't do this."

Wrenching her hand away, she glared at him, all her anger, all the pain and betrayal, rising to the surface. "What do you want from me, absolution? Fine, you've got it. I understand why you did what you did. I *get* it. But you don't understand how much you hurt me! You made me feel . . . not so alone, for the first time in a long, long time. And now I feel more alone than I've ever felt before."

Her voice choking on the last word, Kat turned to go, but Luke again grabbed her arm, standing now as he turned her toward him, his eyes imploring. Kat stiffened, bracing herself for another round even as she closed her eyes against a blur of tears.

"Let her go, honey." Kat started at the sound of Victoria's soft, calming voice from the doorway.

"Yes, let me go," Kat said, her voice only a whisper now, her throat too constricted for anything louder. A breathless moment passed as Luke stared down at her. At last he stepped back from her, raising his arms in resignation.

Kat spun around and headed for the doorway. Victoria stepped aside to let her pass, but Kat stopped in front of her, blinking back her tears. She swallowed hard, forcing her throat to open. "I have an idea how to help you," she told her, her voice raspy and quaking. "I have to talk to my editor first, but I think it'll work. You'd still have to tell Jeremy the truth, though."

Surprise registered on Victoria's face; then she smiled and shrugged. "We were going to anyway." She wrapped her hand gently around Kat's forearm. "Thank you. Anything you could do, we'd appreciate more than you know. And I truly am sorry you were so hurt in all of this."

Kat nodded once, then headed down the hallway toward the stairs, suddenly desperate for the solitude of the cabin.

Chapter Twenty-two

Kat looked around the tiny bedroom of the cabin, then let out a long breath before closing the top of her valise. The *snap* had the sound of finality to it. And that was good, right? To be done with this place?

"Right," she said out loud to the empty room. Glancing down at her watch, she saw that she had plenty of time to get to the airport to catch her flight.

No more private jets for her. The Winslows had needed the Lear for one last ski trip to Switzerland before the end of the season. The Janssens had offered Kat the use of their plane, but she'd refused, wanting to wash her hands of all things Janssen as soon as possible. And so she was slumming her way back to New York on a commercial flight. She had a ticket for the last shuttle of the night from Aspen to Denver International, then the red-eye home. In fact, she was so early, she could drive slowly, enjoy some of the Rocky Mountain scenery she'd missed on her way out here.

Walking into the front room, she put her valise down by the door, then headed to the couch and sat down in front of the coffee table. Running her hand across the bright wool blanket covering the couch, Kat nodded to herself, deciding to do something similar in her condo. She liked the rustic feel of the cabin—the Indian blankets hanging on the walls, the natural rock fireplace, the simple but solid-looking wood furniture.

She was glad she'd come up with an idea to keep her busy during the next month or so—a complete overhaul of her condo. She'd sell or give away her grandmother's clutter and redecorate as *she* wanted it. Maybe then it would feel more like a real home to her.

She'd even sketched out a couple of decorating ideas during her spare time, what little she'd had of it. She'd spent the past week sitting down with Alex, Victoria, and Luke for several long conversations about their lives, all recorded on the Dictaphone Alex had lent her. He'd told her he used it to play back his lines as he rehearsed them.

The Janssens had agreed to have the transcripts of the interviews published at the end of the book, word for word, so nothing could be taken out of context or doctored by tricky editing as Victoria had so greatly feared.

Not surprisingly, Upstairs at Winslow had been thrilled with the idea. "Are you kidding?" Brian had burst out over the phone. "Exclusive rights to the first in-depth Janssen interview in ten years?" And with only a little cajoling, Winslow had even agreed to donate a percentage of the net profits to the cancer ward at Denver Children's Hospital. Kat's idea. Still, they stood to make a fortune off the book.

Hearing a horse whinnying somewhere outside, Kat looked up and sighed. She hadn't gotten a chance to even ride one, much less gallop.

This hadn't been much of a vacation. She'd spent most of her time in this very room, conducting the interviews in the cabin so there'd be no chance of Jeremy's overhearing any of it. Thankfully, he was out of the woods as far as the blood poisoning went, but Alex and Victoria wanted to give him a little more time to recuperate before telling him the truth about his biological father.

Kat leaned toward the coffee table and began carefully placing the miniature Dictaphone tapes in the side pocket of her purse. She wanted to keep them close. Picking up the Dictaphone, she ejected the tape inside, the last of her sessions with Luke. She'd finished with him just that afternoon.

Concerned about his privacy, he'd been reluctant to do it at all in the beginning but had relented when it became clear it would be the best thing for Jeremy. Still, he'd obviously been uncomfortable. As she had been.

From the guilty way he'd looked at her, Kat could tell Luke felt bad about using her as he had, and she knew now he wasn't a terrible person, just desperate to help the nephew he loved so very much. Unfortunately, *she'd* been the one to bear the consequences of his deception.

To his credit, he'd tried to make her time here easier by staying away from her, and she appreciated that. And, after all, he'd already said his "sorry"s her first night here, and she'd forgiven him. There was nothing else for them to say to each other. Now she just needed to convince her heart of that. *It* still had a *lot* to say.

During his interviews Luke had maintained a professional air, being candid and straightforward about his life. He relayed the information in a near monotone, emotionless except for when he'd mentioned the name he and Annie had chosen for their son, Henry. His voice had broken on the last syllable, and he'd fallen quiet for a moment. Kat had quickly made a point of looking intently at her notes, busily scribbling on her pad, but in her peripheral vision she saw him wipe his eyes and swallow hard several times. Seeing that, she'd had to blink back a few tears herself.

In a later session he'd told her how he came to be at the ranch. Bored with his software company, he'd sold it and begun looking to do something new with his life. He'd spent an exciting summer on the ranch after meeting the previous owner at the Denver stock show. The owner had wanted to retire with his wife to Arizona, and Luke had bought the ranch outright from him. And now it was his life.

The horse whinnied again, sounding closer now—very

close, actually. Curious, Kat stood, walked to the door, and opened it.

Immediately she had to raise a hand to shield her eyes from the blazing sun, sitting just above the horizon between two distant mountains.

The horse *was* close—just outside the door, actually— tied to one of the pine trees in the front yard and silhouetted against the late-afternoon sky, brilliant with more shades of red and orange than she'd ever seen.

"That hair of yours gives even a sunset like that a run for its money."

Luke.

Kat squinted through the brightness and saw him standing on the other side of the horse, fiddling with one of the leather saddlebags. The horse shifted slightly to the left, and Kat could make out splotches of color on its flanks. The palomino.

"Pepperjack, meet Kat Callahan." Hearing his name, the horse shook his head and let out a soft grunt. "Kat, meet the best dang galloper on the planet, Pepperjack."

Just then the setting sun passed through a band of clouds low on the horizon, and Kat lowered her hand. Luke had unfastened the flap of the saddlebag and was now pulling something out of it, something familiar. Kat's eyes widened as Luke walked around the horse. Was that . . . ? Yes, her laptop!

"I hope you don't mind," he began, holding it out to her, "but I asked Jessie to grab this too when she picked up Lucy from your condo."

Perplexed, Kat took it from him. "But why?"

Dipping his cowboy hat at her, Luke gave her a half grin very much like his big brother's. "Well, little lady, you don't reckon I'd create that snazzy little virus without a snazzy little vaccine, do you?"

Kat gulped in a breath. "You mean . . ."

Luke nodded. "*The View from Here*. It's all there. Fully intact."

"Wow," was all Kat could think of to say as she clutched the computer to her side. "Thank you." But then she let out an ironic little laugh. "Wait, why am I thanking you?" Her jaw clenched tightly as she remembered all she'd been through, thinking she'd lost her book, all her hard work gone.

For a long moment Luke just looked at her, saying nothing. Kat met his gaze head-on, unflinching. His continuing smile irked her. And was that amusement flickering in his blue eyes?

Finally he shrugged—it was a bit exaggerated, Kat thought.

"Fair enough." He looked down at the ground and kicked a tuft of grass with his boot. "I guess I'll just see you around, then." Turning, he jammed his thumbs into his pockets and began walking back toward the main house.

"Um, excuse me?" Kat called after him, her tone sarcastic. "I think you forgot something?" As Luke turned back to her, Kat nodded pointedly at the horse.

"Oh, no, I didn't," he replied with a mild shrug. And

there was that amused smile again. "He's yours now, whether or not you say yes. If the answer's no, I'm sure Jessie'll be happy to put him up for you. She's already got about twenty or so horses out there on that 'cozy little place' of hers in the Hamptons."

Kat let out a frustrated breath. "What are you talking about?"

Just then the sun passed through the clouds, and there it was again, a glowing red orb lying low and heavy on the horizon behind Luke. Kat again raised a hand to shield her eyes.

Squinting into the brightness, she saw Luke—or the silhouette of him anyway—take another step closer to her, and reflexively she backed up, but the cabin's screen door stopped any further retreat.

Relentless, he came closer, pausing a foot in front of her—so close, he blocked out the sun. She could see his face now, his eyes boring into hers, the amusement gone, his jawline taut with tension.

Being trapped together by the sun's blinding rays gave Kat a surreal feeling, as if they were standing in a universe all their own.

As Luke's gaze dropped to her mouth, Kat felt every muscle in her body tense up. But then she relaxed as she made the decision.

For one last moment she would let him in, accept him into her space. She would let herself fall back into the Kat she'd become with him—a Kat in love.

Already, she knew the ghost of that Kat would haunt her for years to come and knew with equal certainty that she'd never let anyone in as she had him. With him she'd hesitantly tested the waters of love and had been scalded by them, scarred. She'd never take that chance again.

But for those times when she craved that other Kat, for those weak moments she was sure to have, she would think back to this moment and remember it, like passing her finger through the flame of a candle, flirting with the pain, reminding her of the danger beneath the beauty, the warmth.

Kat closed her eyes as she felt Luke's index finger gently touch her under her chin, his thumb caressing just her lower lip. One last kiss, she told herself, for that other Kat.

She opened her eyes and tilted her head up to his, breathing in his scent, committing it to memory.

But Luke suddenly turned away from her, instead nodding over at the horse. "So," he began, his lips curling up in that slow grin of his, "you ever hear of a 'bridal price'?"

Frowning, Kat cocked her head at him and let out a loud, frustrated breath. Now that she'd decided to allow the kiss, she *wanted* it. "What does the cost of a bridle have to do with anything?"

Luke looked surprised and confused but then shook his head, a chuckle sounding from deep in his throat. "No, not *bridle, l-e. Bridal, a-l.*"

Kat had to think about that for a moment, but as his meaning sank in, her heart jumped into overdrive. "You mean . . . as in . . ."

Smiling, Luke nodded. "There are several Native Americans working on the ranch, and they told me about it. It's a tribal custom to bring a gift—such as a horse—when a man comes a-callin' to ask a woman to marry him. I liked the idea. I would have done it earlier, but I didn't want you to be distracted from the interviews."

But Kat was having a hard time paying attention to him. One word had lodged in her head. " 'Marry'?" she whispered, swallowing hard.

Leaving her reeling, Luke took a step back from her and looked out at the horse pasture. Putting two fingers into his mouth, he let out a shrill whistle, and Kat heard a sharp yelp come from somewhere far off in the pasture. Lucy. A moment later Kat saw her bounding toward them across the pasture, then sneaking under the fence and racing across the footbridge.

Several yards away, the Lab slowed and trotted the rest of the way, panting hard. Kat thought she saw something gleam from the Lab's collar and looked closer as Lucy stopped next to Luke, dropping down onto her hind legs. Her tail swishing back and forth on the ground, she looked up at Luke expectantly.

"Good girl," he said, petting her the way she liked. He began fingering her collar—not her usual blue one, though. This one was red—but, wait, that wasn't a collar at all, was it? Kat took a step closer, leaned over, and saw that Luke was untying a bright red ribbon tied around the dog's neck, something dangling off it. . . .

"Oh, my," Kat whispered, as she identified it, falling heavily into Luke's palm. Her entire body felt suddenly limp, wilted.

"Oh, hey there," Luke said, dipping down to grab the laptop hanging precariously in her weakened grip. "I wouldn't want you to drop that." He put it down carefully next to the cabin door, then rose.

"I don't . . ." Kat began, but her voice trailed off as she realized she had no words to follow up with.

He grinned at her. "What, have I actually rendered you speechless?"

Kat nodded, then let out a little laugh when she realized it had only emphasized his point.

Luke's smile faded as he stepped closer to her, his fingers playing with the object he was holding, the thing Kat was trying hard to get her mind around.

"You know," he began softly, looking down into her eyes, "I wasn't lying when I told you I'd read everything you'd written—everything I could find on the Internet anyway, even trade articles. You're a great writer, Kat. You convey thoughts and ideas—even complex ones—clearly, succinctly, eloquently . . . and a lot more-*ly* words I can't think of right now."

He reached up and brushed back a strand of hair that had fallen across her stunned face.

"Your writing . . . I don't know, it *touched* me." A small smile played at the corners of his mouth. "I tried to fight it, not wanting to feel anything for you. You were, after all, the enemy." His lips formed a tender smile, his eyes taking in every inch of her face. "But the fact of it is, I think I fell in love with you months ago, through only your writing. And then I met the woman behind the words, and I was hooked. Hell, I *am* hooked."

Kat swallowed hard, still unable to put even two words together. She realized that as Luke spoke, the *other* Kat was sneaking back, the in-love Kat, and for a moment she tensed, her old defenses cranking up again. But then she relaxed as she felt them slowly diffuse. Some things were worth the risk.

Luke's expression grew serious again. "I admit, we got off to a rocky start. I know I told you a lot of lies, and I'm sorry about that. But please know that when it counted, when it *meant* something, I never once lied to you. And I think you know that."

Kat found herself nodding without even thinking about it, and at last she found her voice. "I do."

At that, Luke's face broke into a broad grin, his eyebrows raised. " 'I do'? Aren't you jumping the gun a little? At least let me do my bit first!"

Kat nodded, letting out a nervous laugh, while at the same time tears welled in her eyes.

And then Luke was taking off his cowboy hat, ruffling his fingers through his flattened curls before dropping down onto one knee. He took her hand and held it gently, looking up into her eyes. "I love you, Kat Callahan." Kat's heart nearly burst in her chest, she'd wanted so badly to hear those words from him, words she'd thought were forever lost to her. "More than anything else in the world I want to spend the rest of my life with you. Will you marry me?"

Just then, Lucy let out a sharp yip, and they both looked at her. She was watching them intently, as if comprehending what was happening. "Great timing, kid," Luke muttered, but he was smiling.

Kat laughed through her tears. "So, what do you think, Luce? Should I? It'd mean your being stuck with old Oliver for a very long time."

Luke looked fondly at his dog. "Oh, I don't think she'd mind that one bit, would you, girl?"

In answer, Lucy let out a joyous-sounding yelp, and Kat gave her a decisive nod. "All right, as long as it's okay with you . . ." She looked back down at Luke and finished softly, "I guess it's okay by me."

"Is that a yes?" Luke asked, feigning a dubious frown.

"Yes, it's a yes!" Kat laughed, new tears streaming down her cheeks.

Holding her breath, she watched Luke take her left hand, hold out the third finger, and slip the ring on, a beautiful square-cut diamond solitaire mounted on a simple platinum band.

"Oh, Tanner, it's perfect!" she gushed, then drew in a sharp breath, her eyes widening as she covered her mouth with her hand. "I mean, Luke!" Smiling, she ran her hand down the side of his face, the diamond glittering in the fading sunlight. "Whoever you are," she said, her voice soft, meant only for him, "I love it. I love *you*."

Luke's eyes lit up at that, and he stood up and wrapped his arms around her waist, pulling her into him, close. "Say it again," he whispered into her ear.

"I love you," she murmured, her hand curling up around his strong, warm neck.

He pulled back from her, his blue eyes drilling into hers, and Kat could see the love there, so vivid, so clear, and she knew without a doubt that it was reflecting right back at him from her own eyes. Reaching up, he gently wiped away the tears from her face with his thumbs. His gaze fell to her mouth, then flicked back up to her eyes.

"Kiss me, then," Luke said, his voice low and urgent.

Kat smiled, grabbed his belt, and pulled him to her. "Yes, sir," she murmured, and she pressed her mouth against his, loving the soft thickness of his lips, surprised again at their smoothness, attached as they were to this rugged, tough cowboy.

Pepperjack let out an indignant grunt then, reminding them in no uncertain terms that he was still there and ready to go.

They broke apart, laughing, and as Kat looked over at the horse, he stomped at the ground twice with his right front hoof.

"Uh-oh," Luke said with a fond smile. "I think somebody's getting a little impatient."

"Hey, I'm ready!" Kat told Pepperjack. "This guy

here's the one holding us up!" She gestured toward Luke with an indifferent wave, and he laughed.

"Well, I'm sorry my proposal of marriage and pledge of everlasting love and devotion got in y'all's way!"

"Oh, we'll get over it," Kat said with a shrug. Laughing, she bent down and picked up the laptop. "Let me put this inside."

Luke walked to the pine tree to untie the reins as Kat stepped inside the cabin. Seeing her valise by the door, Kat smiled and looked down at her watch. "Oh, well," she sang aloud. That was one plane she didn't mind missing.

Still, she'd have to go back to New York to drop the tapes off at Winslow and return Brian's ring to him. For some reason she wasn't dreading that as much as she'd thought. She had the feeling he would be just fine.

She also had to get some things from her condo. It looked as if she'd be extending her stay here a little while longer—by, say, fifty years or so.

She shook her head as the reality of what had just happened began to sink in. Her life would never be the same now. And that was fine with her. This was a much better life, a better *Kat*. And to think she'd come so close to settling for the Kat she'd been only a few minutes earlier, the one who'd been prepared to go back to her old life in New York, an empty life.

Walking to the coffee table to put down the laptop, it occurred to her that she'd saddled her character in *The View from Here* with exactly such a life in the end.

"Don't you worry," she said to her, patting the laptop affectionately. "I'll rescue you."

As she rose and headed back to the cabin door, she caught a glimpse of the ring on her finger and looked at it for a long moment. If not for its cool, heavy presence, she could have convinced herself that this had all been a dream.

Twirling the ring around her finger with her thumb, she headed back to the door, her heart swelling in her chest, pulsing with emotion she felt still growing inside her. She had no idea where it would stop. And at the moment, her capacity for love—to love and to *be* loved—seemed boundless.

Back outside, she saw Luke standing by Pepperjack's head, stroking his elegant neck.

"You know, I'm going to have to change the ending of my book now," she told him, closing the door behind her.

"Oh, yeah?" Luke smiled at her as he stepped to the side of the horse and, in one smooth motion, swung himself easily up into the saddle. Kat walked to Pepperjack, her heart rate quickening at the thought that, in just a couple of minutes, she'd be fulfilling her long-held dream.

"I don't want her to be alone in the end."

"No?" Luke asked, leaning over to help her up. Once settled closely behind him, she wrapped her arms around his warm, muscled belly, savoring the feel of him. He made a little clucking sound with his tongue, and they started forward.

"Nope," Kat continued, moving with the motion of the horse as Luke steered Pepperjack toward the pasture. The sun was making its final descent now, the horizon beginning to swallow it up, a thin slice of it already gone from the underside. "I think some big, strong cowboy—" She stopped, laughing and leaned in closer to his ear. "Or some boring software developer . . ." She felt him chuckle as they clip-clopped across the footbridge. "Will swoop down into her boring city-girl life, create sheer havoc in it—"

" 'Havoc,' huh?" Luke asked, smiling at her over his shoulder as he leaned down to unfasten the pasture gate.

"Yes, *havoc*. A lot of havoc."

Laughing, Luke guided Pepperjack into the pasture and refastened the gate behind them.

"*Anyway*," Kat continued as they headed farther into the pasture. "He'll drag her out West, kicking and screaming. . . ."

Again, Luke peered back at her, one eyebrow raised. " 'Kicking and—' "

"Screaming," Kat finished perfunctorily. "And then—"

"Wait, let me guess," Luke interrupted, turning Pepperjack toward the west, just the fiery top of the sun still visible along the horizon, although the sky above it had grown even more spectacular than before, ablaze with ever-deepening shades of scarlet and burnt orange. "They ride off into the sunset?" He gave her a skeptical look over his shoulder. "A bit clichéd, isn't it?"

"Oh, but there's a difference," Kat said, her voice enticing. She reached up, swiped off Luke's hat, and plunked it down on her own head. It was a little big, but it would have to do until she got her own.

Taking in an excited breath, she lifted her heels off the sides of the horse and struck them against his flanks as she'd seen in the movies—not hard, but Pepperjack got the message.

She felt something give beneath her, and as Luke raised his hands, allowing Pepperjack free rein, Kat felt the strong muscles under her flex and contract, all working in perfect harmony, designed for one purpose. Speed.

"They don't just *ride* into the sunset," she said, raising her voice above the wind against her ears.

Luke looked back at her smiling, thrilled face, and he too raised his chin up into the onrushing air and yelled with her, "They *gallop!*"

Epilogue

With a flourish, Kat inserted the last of the wedding pictures into her album. Finally. Between the final rewrites of the book and the book tour, the year since the wedding had been so hectic, she just hadn't found the time. But now at last she was done.

Looking up toward the western sky, she saw the blazing sun sitting a few inches above the horizon.

She was sitting on the porch of the ranch's main house, slowly rocking back and forth on the swing Luke had built months before. "These stupid chairs aren't big enough for two people," he'd complained about the Adirondacks and so had constructed and hung the swing, wide enough for two, in the northwest corner of the porch so that they could watch the sunsets together. That had become something of a tradition for them, and Kat thought she would never tire of it, a different show every night.

Looking back down at the wedding album, Kat opened it to the first page and began leafing through it, smiling as she relived the scenes captured in each photo. And there had certainly been enough of them. Victoria had gone a little camera-happy throughout the whole crazy business, from visiting Aspen incognito to help Kat pick out a wedding gown to seeing them off at the airport for their honeymoon in Florence. But Kat didn't need pictures to remember any of it.

It had been a dream wedding, a simple ceremony set among an abundance of wildflowers in a meadow on the east side of the ranch, one with a particularly stunning view of the magnificent mountain she'd mistaken for a cloud her first night there.

Victoria had been Kat's maid of honor, while Alex did double duty, giving away the bride as well as serving as Luke's best man. Jeremy, now in full remission, proudly served as ring bearer. He'd taken his task very seriously, banning all jokes concerning any losing of the rings. And of course, Tanner—the real one—and Tillie, the ranch cook, had been there.

In the past year Kat had grown to love all of them as family. Tanner had been the most difficult to get to know—a quiet, reserved man everyone liked and re-spected, every word from him well thought out and de-liberate, as if there were a shortage of them and he had to ration them. She'd learned to appreciate that about him and to make a point of listening intently whenever he spoke. Under his charge, the day-to-day operations of the ranch ran as smoothly as a well-lubricated engine.

And then there was Tillie, a woman Kat's grandmother would have called handsome. Rustic, proud, and independent, Kat could easily imagine her as one of the first courageous frontierswomen if she'd lived a century or so earlier.

Kat turned the page and sighed happily at the sight of her favorite photo, the only one Alex Janssen had shot. He'd taken it as they'd all headed back to the house for the reception, Kat and Luke walking hand in hand several yards ahead of everyone else.

Victoria had wanted to call out to Luke and Kat to tell them to turn around and smile for the camera, but Alex had stopped her. Kat was glad he did. She loved the picture precisely because it *wasn't* planned, their postures natural, not stiff and self-conscious as in all the posed shots.

There was something in the subtle tilt of their bodies toward each other, the soft angle of their necklines, the comfortable clasp of their hands, that perfectly captured the intimacy between them, the love. They hadn't been talking, Kat remembered, both just reveling in the joy of the day and their new bond of marriage.

That joy hadn't ended in the year since the wedding but instead had grown and deepened in ways she'd never anticipated. Kat no longer questioned it, where it would end. It still seemed boundless to her.

As for the Janssen book, Upstairs had been right. It did indeed soar up the *New York Times* best-seller list, remaining at number one longer than anyone had anticipated. Winslow had even found a good PR angle in donating so much money to the children's hospital. It had been so much, in fact, that it, combined with the huge sums donated by the Janssens' fans, had enabled the hospital to reopen a previously closed wing, calling it the Cricket Center for the Treatment of Leukemia. A nearby housing facility was also being built for family members of patients treated at the center.

The Janssens had been blindsided by their fans' reaction to the book and their story. As soon as the book hit the shelves, flowers by the truckload had come, dozens of bouquets from well-wishers the world over.

Outwardly Jeremy had scoffed at the flowers, calling them "girly," but everyone knew he was deeply touched by them. And it wasn't just flowers. In addition to mailbags full of get-well cards, he'd been sent enough stuffed animals to fill fifty pretend zoos. He kept saying he was too old for them, but whenever Kat looked in on him at night, he'd be clutching one of them tightly to his side.

And despite everything, the Janssen book had proved to be the means to the end of having a "real" book published after all. Winslow had agreed to publish *The View from Here* under their more literary imprint, Russet Books. It would be coming out in a few months, at which time Kat would have to go on another book tour, although obviously on a much smaller scale than the one for the Janssen book. No Matt Lauer this time around.

Still, though, she might have to cut it short. . . .

Hearing the dogs bark, she looked up to see Oliver and Lucy bounding down the gravel road, followed by Luke on his horse, Sophie, grown now from the adorable foal that had once broken his nose.

Racing ahead, the dogs flew up the driveway and scrambled up the porch steps. They ran down to Kat's corner, their nails clicking against the wooden slats of the porch. Flailing, a little out of control on the smooth paint, they skidded to a stop in front of her, panting hard.

"Hi, guys!" Kat pet each of them in turn and got slobbery, wet kisses from them both. "Ew," she grimaced as she pushed them away, wiping her face. "I already took a bath today! Go away now—play or something!"

Obligingly, they took off, back toward the porch steps and down them, almost tripping Luke as he tied Sophie to the post at the bottom of the steps. Once in the front yard, the dogs began playing in earnest, jumping all over each other, letting out little yips and yelps as they wrestled.

After being cooped up for so long in Kat's condo, Oliver was having the time of his life living on the ranch with its wide-open spaces and all manner of small critters to flush out and chase around. And of course there was Lucy. The two of them had become absolutely inseparable.

"Hey, you almost missed it!" she called to Luke with a nod toward the sunset. He came up the stairs and headed down the porch, spurs clanging noisy and metallic with each step.

Sitting down beside her, he planted a light kiss on her lips, then glanced down at the wedding album in Kat's lap and chuckled. It was opened to a picture of Jeremy wearing a black cowboy hat, his mouth, nose, and cheeks completely covered with white frosting and cake.

Jeremy had urged Kat and Luke to "smush cake" on each other during the traditional first bite of wedding cake, but instead, in perfect unison, as if they'd rehearsed it, they'd both taken a piece and smeared it across *his* face. He'd screamed with laughter.

Lord, how she loved that kid. She'd never thought she'd even have a niece or nephew, and now she couldn't imagine her life without him.

He'd surprised them all when Victoria had nervously told him the truth about Luke's being his biological father just before the book's release.

"Wow, you did all that just to make me?" he'd asked, impressed, but then he'd frowned, turning to Alex. "But you're still Dad, right?"

"Absolutely," Alex had affirmed, ruffling his son's thick dark hair.

"Cool!" Jeremy had responded and immediately turned back to his Xbox.

Luke took Kat's hand now, and for a moment they sat in silence, staring out at the sky as the sunset began to take shape before them, the wispy white-gray clouds along the horizon aglow in shades of pink and rose—what her mother used to call a "pink sky." Kat thought seeing it here between the mountains infinitely more satisfying than catching glimpses of it through towering skyscrapers.

She sensed Luke looking at her and turned to him. With a tender smile, he whispered, "I love you, you know."

Kat smiled and leaned into him, pressing her lips against his, holding the kiss a beat longer than she'd intended. "You too."

Her gaze fell to Pepperjack standing in the field across from them, his flanks lit up by the blazing sunset, his head bent as he muzzled the grass. Kat closed the wedding album and held it to her chest. She could feel her heart beating hard and fast against it. "You know," she began, affecting a casual tone, "I'm going to have to get as much galloping in as possible over the next couple of weeks."

Out of the corner of her eye, she saw Luke's quizzical look.

"Well," Kat explained after a dramatic sigh, "the doctor says it's not a good idea after the first trimester." Instantly the swing stopped as Luke planted his boots on the porch below them, the spurs' loud *clang* speaking volumes.

Glancing over at him, Kat laughed. His mouth was literally gaping open. He swallowed hard. "Tri—what?"

"Oh, I think you heard me," Kat said in a singsong voice.

"Wow," was all Luke said. Standing, he walked to the porch railing, planted his hands down on it, raised his head, and let out a "Yee-haw!" so loud, Pepperjack and Jeremy's horse, Lemondrop, standing far off in the horse pasture, raised their heads in unison.

His eyes shining with excitement, Luke came back over to her, sat down, and pressed his hand gently across her belly, even though it was still completely flat. "Well, now, little lady," he began, and now, instead of irritating her, Kat laughed at his aw-shucks accent. "That thar's something we've been sorely lackin' 'round here—a redheaded cowpoke."

Kat grinned, covering his hand with her own. "Or pokette." Then she frowned thoughtfully, gazing out at the sky, now deep crimson and scarlet. "Or maybe he— or she—will be a computer nerd."

Luke shrugged. "Or a writer."

"Or an artist," Kat suggested, thinking of her father.

Luke chuckled. "Heck, why not *D*, all of the above? *And* President of the United States?"

"Okay," Kat said simply, and she rested her head against Luke's strong shoulder. He put his arm around her and pulled her close.

Done with playing at last, the exhausted dogs came up from the front yard, moving more slowly now as they headed down the porch, collapsing in front of the swing.

Kat sighed, as contented as she'd ever been in her

life, soaking in the perfection of the moment—the warm, balmy air; the enticing smell of the roast wafting through the open window behind them; the clanging of metal and china as Tillie prepared what promised to be a wonderful meal.

Kat could just make out, too, Jeremy's joyous giggling, coming from upstairs. Yes, what a wonderful sound a child's laugh was, she thought. She couldn't wait to hear her own child's first giggle, see the first smile, the first step. . . . So much to look forward to.

Kat closed her eyes, and instantly an image appeared in her mind's eye—she and Luke sitting here still, decades from now, watching their grandchildren frolic in the front yard as the dogs had, all of them happy and loved, against the backdrop of yet another spectacular Colorado sunset.